GIVING MY HEART TO A RUDE BOY

VEE BRYANT

SHAN PRESENTS, LLC

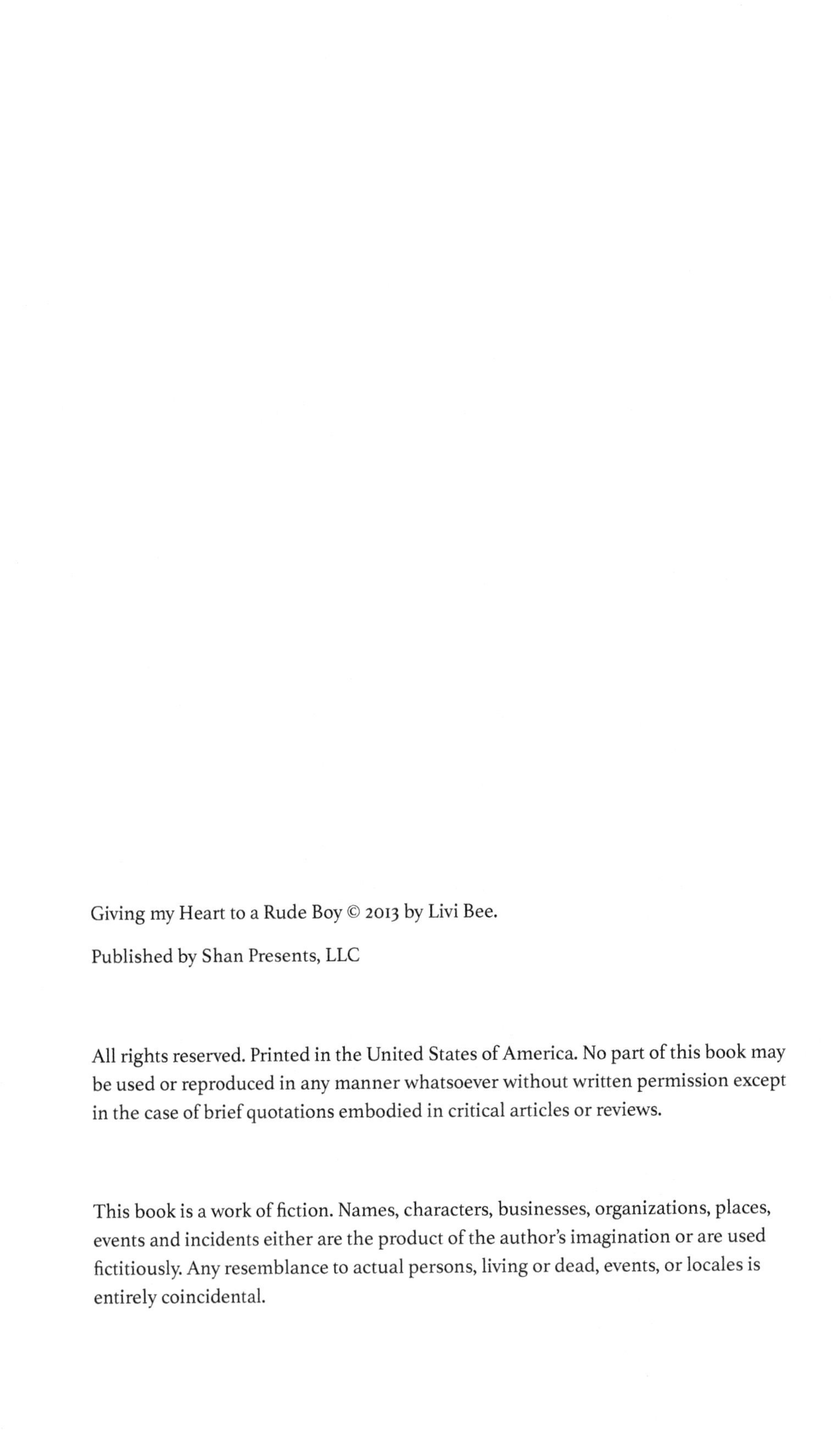

Published by Shan Presents, LLC

ACKNOWLEDGMENTS

I would like to thank God. He's the reason I'm still writing. At one point, I was ready to give up, but I prayed and God reminded me that he's got me. I would like to thank all the authors who support me, too. It really means a lot to me knowing there are other authors who are going through the same thing as I am. My family, without the support of my loved ones, I wouldn't be me. They encourage me to do better. My boyfriend, Leonard Lyons, is the absolute best.

I would like to thank my first publisher, A. Lynn. She's great and helped me out a lot. I wish her all the best in her writing career. This process has shown me to follow my dreams, you never know what the outcome might be.

My Mother, who's my queen, I have to give thanks to her for the simple reason, I love her. She supports me and I'm trying to make her proud.

UNTITLED

Text Shan to 22828 to stay up to date with new releases, sneak peeks, contest, and more...

Or sign up Here

Check your spam if you don't receive an email thanking you for signing up.

PROLOGUE

W*HAP! WHAP!*

I felt the stinging, hard slaps in my sleep. I frantically awakened from my sleep.

"What the fuck were you doing in the club, ma?" Kyson, my boyfriend of three years, asked. But before I could answer, he punched me in my mouth, instantly drawing blood.

I caught him with his hoes once again. But, of course, I was in the wrong for being out with my friends.

"Stay the fuck out of the club!" Kyson yelled, snatching me up so that we were face-to-face. "Do you hear me?"

When he pinned me up against the wall in our bedroom, I frantically nodded as tears escaped from my eyes.

Here I was like a dumb ass, letting him cheat, beat, and belittle me. I was too weak to stand up for myself.

"Go fix me some breakfast," he gritted as he turned and walked upstairs to a crying Dalilah as if he hadn't just beat my ass.

I shook my head and cried. I was so tired of this shit, but what was I going to do about it? Leave? I doubted it. Hurt him back? I tried it, but it only made the ass whooping worse. If my stupid ass would've just listened to my mother, maybe I wouldn't be in this predicament. I wish I would have never spoken to this nigga in that corner store when I was seventeen. I was young and dumb. I let the fact that he had money and a nice smile, lure me in and I'd been stuck ever since.

1

DIAMOND

Three Years Earlier...

It was a hot, sweaty day in Compton, California. That day was my seventeenth birthday and I was with my best friend, Keisha. I was dressed in a pair of True Religion jeans, a pink crop top, and a pair of pink sandals. My long, honey blonde hair was pulled into a high ponytail.

"Why the fuck is it so hot outside?" I asked as I sat on the bench at the bus stop. We were on our way to Long Beach Plaza and Mini Mall. I needed a dress for my birthday dinner that night.

"Girl, you know how California weather is," Keisha said, but I didn't respond. My attention was across the street looking at Kyson, who was a local dope boy. Everyone knew him but he didn't hang with many. I had a thing for him and didn't know why. Maybe it was his chocolate skin or the way he smiled every time I saw him. Before I knew it, I was rushing across the street towards the store. I wanted to meet him. I'd heard so many things about him. Keisha and I walked in and immediately all eyes were on us.

"Wassup, ma?" he asked, flashing his million-dollar smile.

I was nervous. I didn't expect him to acknowledge me, let alone speak to me. But I smiled back and said hello.

He looked me up and down and licked his lips, causing chills to run down my body, a feeling I'd never get from anyone else.

"Where are you ladies headed on this hot ass day?" he asked, causing Keisha and I both to giggle.

"The mall. Today's her birthday," Keisha chimed in.

I nudged her in the arm and looked at her because she didn't know this man to be telling him our business.

"Ouch!" she yelped in pain.

Kyson and his friend looked at each other then back at us.

"Roll with me today?" he asked. Without even waiting for me to answer, he grabbed my hand and walked me to his black Camaro. After opening my door for me, I stepped in.

I watched as Keisha climbed into the car with his friend and we drove off.

"How old are you?" Kyson asked as he eyed my thick thighs.

"Seventeen."

I was so certain that he would stop his car and put me out. But instead, he continued the drive towards the mall. I felt his eyes on me, so I turned his way.

"What are you looking at?"

He was making me feel uncomfortable. He smiled but didn't say anything. I was ditching his ass as soon as we hit the mall because he could be a killer for all I knew. But if he was a killer, he was the sexiest murderer I had ever seen, dressed in some black Levi's, a white T-shirt, and a pair of white Air Force Ones. I couldn't keep my eyes off his dick print, either. Just because I was a virgin didn't mean that I was blind and from what I saw, he was blessed.

Once we entered Long Beach Plaza, I checked my phone for the time because I didn't want to be late for my dinner and have my mother pissed at me. It was already going on six in the evening. I tried walking away from him but he grabbed my hand.

"Could you not?" I asked, trying to pull my hand away but he wouldn't let it go.

He looked at me and smiled. "Why you so nervous, ma? I'm not going to hurt you."

I calmed down and walked with him. For some reason, I believed him. We were getting dirty looks from everyone. I knew it was because he was so much older than I was.

"You ready to shop?" he asked, ignoring the looks bitches were giving him.

When I nodded, he took me into several stores and balled out on me. Half of the shit I wouldn't be caught dead in because it was too expensive.

I didn't understand why he didn't have a problem with spending his money on me. He must've did this with all his women. I was standing in the dressing room, trying on a dress for my dinner and it was beautiful. It was a floor-length, illusion and lace dress made by Jovani. Looking at the price tag, I knew I couldn't afford it. So, I took it off, placed it back on the hanger, and walked out of the store. Kyson walked quietly behind me to his car and placed the bags into the trunk. He got in and we drove in silence.

"Where you live at, ma?" he asked, looking at his phone then me.

I really didn't want him to see my neighborhood but at that point, I really had no other choice.

"I live in Sunny Clove."

He looked at me and smiled. "I grew up out there. Does Momma Cha still live out there?"

I laughed thinking about Momma Cha. That woman was like the grandma of the hood. Somebody bothering you? You went to get Momma Cha. That woman was a fool.

"Yeah, where her crazy ass going?" I said as we both laughed.

The entire ride we got to know each other and I learned he was twenty-four-years-old, graduated top of his college class, and had no kids. He also informed me that he worked in the streets but without actually saying, "I sell drugs for a living." He owned his own home and he didn't seem like the flashy type at all. I was truly intrigued by him. I didn't want the day to end but I knew I had to go and get ready.

When he pulled up to my house, of course, my brother and his simpleminded wannabe thug friends would be sitting on the porch. I climbed out of the car with Kyson right behind me. He had my bags in both of his hands.

"You okay here by yourself?"

I nodded. He kissed my cheek and hugged me before we exchanged phone numbers and he left. I couldn't wait to fill Keisha in on what happened.

Walking into the restroom, I turned the shower on and decided to call Keisha while I waited for the water to get hot. The phone rang twice before she picked up.

"Hey, Poochie," she answered, calling me by my nickname from when I was younger.

I rolled my eyes and laughed. "Bitch, don't call me that."

"You know I'm always going to call you that. But, wassup? Are you getting ready?" she asked.

"I'm about to get into the shower but I had to call and tell you about my shopping spree that Kyson took me on."

"A shopping spree?" she asked.

I smiled like she could see me. "Bitch, you should see my closet."

I heard her giggling. "Los, stop."

"Bitch, bye," I laughed and hung up.

After taking a shower, I styled my hair into spiral curls and walked out of the restroom. I was surprised to see Talia and Keisha.

"Um, can I get dressed?"

They walked out of the room. I dried off, put some cocoa butter on my body, and proceeded to get dressed. I decided on a black high waisted skirt and a pink blouse. I let my curls down and slipped my feet into some nude Christian Louboutins patent pumps that belonged to my mother. I did a double take in my full body length mirror and couldn't believe the way I looked. My caramel skin tone was glistening. Some say I reminded them of the rapper Honey Cocaine, just a shorter version.

I grabbed my iPhone 5s, Gucci clutch, and walked out of my bedroom.

"Damn, D, you look beautiful," Keisha beamed.

"Thanks, boo, you looking gorgeous yourself."

She was dressed in a black, low-cut sheer dress with black faux suede strappy peep toe heels. Her jet-black hair was pulled into a neat bun and she wore heart shaped diamond studs. Talia walked in the house with a sly smile on her face.

"What?"

"I hope you don't mind us inviting Nadia."

When she said that, my entire face dropped. "Of course not. She only slept with and got pregnant by my boyfriend," I said sarcastically.

"Play nice please," Keisha pleaded, linking our arms as we walked out of the house.

"It's my day not hers I'm not doing shit."

Stepping outside, Kyson and Los were posted up by their cars.

"Damn, where y'all going?" my brother's baby mother, Toni, asked.

I ignored her on purpose because I didn't fuck with her at all.

"What time you coming home?" Demarcus asked.

I shrugged my shoulders. I didn't understand why he cared so much.

"Nah, I need a better answer than that," he demanded.

"Look, I don't know. I might stay at Keisha's house," I stated as I made my way to Kyson's car. Once Kyson got in, we drove off.

"Are you really going to stay with Keisha?" he asked, intertwining his hand in mine.

I shrugged. "I only said that because I had no idea when I'd be back."

"Nah, you're coming home with me."

I smiled but said nothing. I had no plans of going home with Kyson. The drive was quiet and I had no idea where we were headed. Looking out the window, he pulled into a restaurant that was located in the boondocks. Once the car came to a complete stop, he got out then came over to my side and opened the door.

"Where are we?"

"Do you trust me?" he asked.

"I don't trust anybody."

He smiled as we walked into the restaurant.

"Table for eight," Kyson said.

Los, Keisha, Talia, Terrance, my mother, and Nadia were going to be dining with us.

A few minutes later, we sat at the table and looked over the menu in silence while we waited for Keisha and Los.

"Wassup bro? My bad, we got busy," Los said when they arrived ten minutes later.

I couldn't help but laugh.

"I see," I said as I nodded towards his unzipped pants and looked at Keisha in total disbelief and shock.

How could she give it up so fast like that? She shrugged her shoulders and sat down next to me. I could feel Kyson staring at me so I turned his way.

"Why do you keep staring at me but not say anything?"

I was tired of his grown ass playing games.

"Because you're so beautiful, Diamond."

I blushed and had butterflies in my stomach. "Thanks, handsome."

The waitress walked back to the table, smacking her gum and staring at Kyson like she knew him.

"What can I get y'all to drink?" she asked.

"Let me get a bottle of your finest wine," Kyson said.

The waitress looked at me then around the table at everyone else.

"Mmhmm, alright."

This chick was so ghetto that it wasn't even funny. Keisha looked sideways and said, "Bitch, just go get what the fuck he asked for and stop staring at us."

I rolled my eyes. I didn't see why Keisha always had to get out of character for these hoes. "Kee, chill," Los said while placing his hand on hers and for the first time, I saw the love she had for this nigga that she just met.

I hoped she was being smart about her shit and not trusting that nigga. He could be faithful, but Momma Cha always told me, "Niggas gone always be niggas. Ya hear me?"

"Diamond, you ready to order?" Kyson's voice brought me back to reality.

"Yes, I'd like the baked potato, grilled fish, shrimp, and a salad."

The rest of them ordered.

"It'll be out in a few. Holla if you need me," the waitress said.

I looked at Kyson and smirked. "Is something funny, sweetheart?"

"The fact that this nigga sitting here with your young ass is funny."

I looked at the girl. She was thick and pretty and looked just like Toccara from America's Top Model. I chuckled but still didn't respond. I was taught to act like a lady and think like a boss. I couldn't give that bitch control but Lord knows I wanted to get up from that table and give her a piece of my mind as she walked away without another word.

"Girl, you better than me because I would've beaten her ass," Keisha said.

Twenty minutes later, the waitress walked over with our food.

"It's about time. A nigga starving," Los laughed.

As she passed our food around, I watched as she touched Kyson's manhood. He was disrespecting me by not saying anything, so I did it for him.

"Excuse me, that man you're touching doesn't belong to you."

Kyson smiled and pushed the thirsty little hoe back. This nigga was waiting on me to say something, but I had nothing to say. As we started eating, we all began to make small talk. I was ready to see what else we were doing that night.

We finished eating, paid, and walked out of the restaurant.

"What you want to do now?" Kyson asked.

"I don't know it's going on eight, though.

"So? The night is just beginning."

"First, I need to get out of this dress and I want to go to the beach," I said.

"Whatever my Queen wants, she shall receive," Kyson charmed.

He was so polite and respectful for a street nigga. Getting into his car, we drove towards the mall.

"What are we doing here?" I asked as I sat back, I wasn't getting out.

"Get out!" he yelled.

I sighed but got out anyway.

"We look like we just left prom," I joked.

He put his arm around my waist and pulled me to his side. As we walked through the mall, I saw this pretty pink two-piece that I wanted with matching black Armani sandals.

"That's it," I picked it up and then waited for him to get his swimming trunks.

When we got to the register, the girl behind the counter gave me the most unpleasant look.

"Would this be all for you?" the chick asked, smiling and flirting with Kyson.

I didn't say anything and neither did he. After he paid for our items, we left the mall.

"Why all these bitches be staring at you?" I asked, eyeing Kyson up and down. I wondered what he had that made those ugly birds go crazy.

"Because you have me and they don't. The moment I saw you, I knew I was making you my girl."

I was stunned by his words. "Oh, yeah?"

"Listen, I don't have a reason to lie. I'm not trying to get in your panties, either. Just say you'll give me a chance to prove all those doubts you have wrong," he said with pleading eyes.

I didn't understand why he was so sure about this. I mean, I liked him but this was our first date.

"I don't know, Kyson."

When my cell phone started ringing, I looked at the caller ID to see that it was my mother calling and answered it.

"Where are you going Diamond Nyla?" My mother asked.

I looked at Kyson, who was staring at me with that same goofy ass smile. I sucked my teeth and said, "The beach with some friends."

My mother let out a long sigh. "Alright, have fun."

I looked at my phone when I heard a clicking sound, indicating that she hung up.

"What?" he smiled when I looked at him.

For some reason, I wanted to feel his lips and I wanted to feel his strong arms around my waist. I shook those thoughts off as fast as they came.

The drive to the beach wasn't as long as I thought it would be. We drove around, looking for somewhere to park.

"Why are all of these people here?" I asked Keisha who was all in Los's face.

"Bae, come on," Kyson said as he grabbed my hand.

To say I was really starting to like him was an understatement. As I walked beside Kyson, I was getting looks of jealousy and hate.

"Let's get in the water," I said while removing my shorts and shirt.

"Damn, you bad as fuck," An unknown man said while looking directly in between my legs.

Kyson stood in front of me. "You see something you like?"

I was praying this nigga didn't say yes. But, his dumb ass nodded and smirked.

"Actually, I do."

I heard Kyson chuckle. "Nah, that belongs to me."

I was upset. I wasn't property. I belonged to Jeanette Carter and Freddy Carter.

"Excuse me but I don't belong to anyone. I'm not property, I'm a person.," I said and walked away, leaving both of them standing there like fools.

There were a few guys and girls playing beer bong so I decided to play, too.

"Can I play?" I asked one of the guys.

"Hell yeah, come and get on my team," he said.

I obliged and we started one hell of a game.

"Okay, it's your turn. You ready?" the cutie asked.

"Wait, what's your name?"

"Christian. What's yours?"

I threw my ball and it landed in a cup. "I'm Diamond."

I spotted Kyson watching me so I smiled at him and he returned the smile and motioned for me to come over to him.

"I have to go. It was nice meeting you Christian," I said and walked off.

Walking towards Kyson, I spotted some chicks all in his and Los's face. I wasn't mad or anything, I just didn't appreciate him flaunting it in my face. The girl who was flirting with Kyson wasn't even cute. She was tall as fuck, at least six feet, had a curly fro, and I wasn't hating or exaggerating but she looked like Kevin Hart. I couldn't be mad.

"Who the fuck is that in my man's face?" A pissed off Keisha asked.

I looked her up and down. "It's not that serious, Keisha," I said, making my way over to Kyson.

I didn't see why she was so insecure so soon. Los must've put it down on her. I smiled at Kyson, who was staring right back at me.

"Wassup, ma?" he said as he grabbed my hand and pulled me close to him.

"Shit. I missed you."

He smiled. "I missed you, too."

Whoever the chick that was standing beside us, looked upset.

"Kyson? Who is this?" the chick asked.

I smiled and put my hand around his waist. "I'm his girlfriend, sweetie. Who are you?"

"I'm his ex-girlfriend," she said, snottily.

I couldn't help but laugh. She thought that it would make me mad.

"Jasmine, get the fuck out of here with all of that," Kyson commanded the girl.

She huffed and walked off, but not before bumping into me.

"I swear the way bitches been coming after me today, you would think me and this nigga been together for a few years," I said before releasing a loud laugh, causing the girl to turn around.

"Bitch, you ain't even in my league!"

Kyson stepped in front of me and looked at Jasmine. "Get the fuck on, hoe!" he yelled.

"I'm ready to go," I said.

"Why? Don't let her ruin your birthday."

"That's not why I'm ready to go," I said.

He grabbed my hand and gave Los a hand dap and brief hug while I hugged Keisha. When we walked away and headed towards the car, we were approached by three young boys.

"We need some work," one of the boys bluntly said.

Kyson didn't acknowledge them. Instead, he walked me to the passenger's side and opened the door for me. After I got in, he shut the door and walked away with the young boys. I heard a few muffled noises before Kyson ran back to the car in a hurry and sped into traffic. I had no idea what was going on. All I knew was that I wanted to take a shower and go to bed.

"Are you hungry?" he asked.

I nodded while hanging onto the door for support. He made his way to the Golden Star, a Chinese restaurant that wasn't far from the beach. When we arrived, we got vegetable egg rolls and a combination of beef, chicken, and shrimp fried rice, then made our way to his house.

The drive was awkward so I pulled out my phone and shot Keisha a message to inform her that I was staying with Kyson while she let me know that she was staying with Los.

I smiled and flipped my phone face down. I felt Kyson's eyes on me but I didn't say anything. Once we made it to his house, I was in awe. This nigga's house was huge with a front lawn manicured to perfection. The cars he had sitting in the driveway were a 2012 white Bentley, a 2014 black Ferrari, and a 2013 black Tahoe. But, I thought it was kind of weird that the house was black brick. It was plain, too.

He parked, grabbed the food and drinks, and we stepped out of the car.

After unlocking it, I pushed the heavy wooden door open and my heart almost dropped. I immediately admired the blue and white décor. He sat the food on the kitchen counter and gave me a tour.

"This is ours."

I giggled and he gave me the sexist puppy dog eyes.

"Like I was saying, this is our living room, kitchen, double office, and right down those stairs lead to my man cave where I spend the majority of my time."

We walked upstairs and he showed me three guest rooms that had king sized beds and flat screens in them. Walking further down the hallway, we reached a pair of double door. He pushed them open and led me into what I assumed was his bedroom that was decorated in all white. His king-sized bed was decorated in black Chanel sheets and a black Chanel comforter with too many pillows.

"Now what are you going to do with all of these pillows?" I asked as I pulled some of them off the bed until he tackled me.

He laid between my legs and kissed my lips. I tried to stop the moan from escaping my mouth it felt so good.

"Mmmh."

I wrapped my legs around his waist. For some reason, I wanted to have feelings for whoever I gave my virginity to.

"You're not ready, ma," he said, sitting up and pulling me on top of him.

"Let's go take a shower."

I stood up from the bed and started making my way to his private bathroom. Walking in, I turned the shower on and was about to undress before Kyson walked in.

"Just shower. I have to go make a run," he turned around and walked out of the bathroom.

I didn't understand what was so important that he had to leave me at his house by myself. Shrugging my shoulders I finished undressing and stepped into the hot water. The ringing of my phone snapped me out of my thoughts. Jumping out, I ran into the bedroom to get it. Looking at the screen, it was Keisha.

"Hello," I answered as I sat on the sink counter.

"Hey, girl. Did you enjoy yourself today?"

"Yes, I did. Thanks for coming to dinner with us."

"No doubt, girl."

"What you doing, hoe?" I asked.

"I'm with Los for tonight."

I smiled because we were all creeping and if any of our parents found out, we would all be grounded for life. My mother already thought Keisha was a bad influence for me when I still had straight A's and was getting offers from colleges such as Duke and Yale.

"Have fun, girl. I'm going to let you go so I can take a shower," I said and hung up.

I got back into the shower and took the longest shower ever. I must have scrubbed myself a dozen times. Stepping out, I grabbed a big towel, dried off, and threw my hair into a messy bun. I walked up to his dresser and pulled the drawer open. The nigga had condoms for days in that bitch. I grabbed some of Kyson's boxers and one of his T-shirts that read Brooklyn and put them on. I walked out of the bedroom and down the stairs when I heard some girls laughing along with some guys.

"Yo, who are you?" A thick Nicki Minaj looking chick asked.

I looked her up and down and continued into the kitchen without saying a word.

"Okay, she's a bitchy one," another girl laughed.

She was a dark-skinned and very beautiful.

I fixed a plate of food and sat at the kitchen table. I was just minding my own business when one of the guys walked in and sat next to me.

"What's up, ma?" A guy who looked a lot like Kyson asked while putting his hand on my thigh.

I was already tired of the bullshit.

"I'm Diamond. Do you have the slightest clue where Kyson is?" I asked as I stood up from the table.

I had lost my appetite all of a sudden. I heard the front door open and shut.

"Aye, Diamond!" I heard Kyson yell.

I walked into the living room and he pulled me into his embrace.

"You ate?"

I nodded.

"She a damn lie, bro. She threw that food away!"

Kyson looked at me and pointed for me to follow him upstairs and I obliged.

"What they do?" he asked, causing me to laugh.

"The bright chick with the lopsided booty was rude and the one who looks like you touched my thigh."

Kyson frowned and jumped up and made his way downstairs.

"Nigga, don't touch her again!" he yelled.

The dude looked at me and then Kyson. "She's fine as fuck. Leave her around me and I'm gone fuck your bitch."

Without warning, Kyson swung and his fist connected with the dude's face. The two girls and the other dude thought that shit was funny but I didn't.

"Kyson, chill!" I said as I pulled him off his friend.

We walked back upstairs and he fell back on the bed and stared up at the ceiling, I laid next to him and remained silent. He rolled on top of me and kissed my lips as he then slid his tongue into my mouth. He pulled my shirt over my head and attacked my nipples. He began licking and flicking them with his tongue.

"Oh, shit," I moaned as he started to travel down to my kitty, but not before standing and pulling his boxers off. Before I knew it, his head was between my legs. I felt his tongue on my pearl and I started to pant and squirm. I was trying to get away from him but he held me down and started fucking me with his tongue. Before I knew it, my legs were shaking and I was cumming all over his face. He didn't complain and neither did I.

I lay there, out of breath and sleepy as hell. I thought if he made me do that using just his tongue, I could only imagine what the dick game like. My eyes were starting to get heavy so I rolled over, put one of my legs over his, and closed my eyes.

2

KYSON

I sat and watched Diamond sleep. I couldn't believe that I finally had her exactly where I wanted her. My baby cousin, Talia, used to stay telling me about how Diamond liked a nigga but my cousin didn't know I felt the same way. I just couldn't fuck with her, though. Shit, her brother and I were beefing. But, when I saw her in the store earlier, I knew it was then or never. So, I took my chance and there she was, baby girl was feeling me just as much as I was feeling her. Her cell phone started ringing so I walked over to her side and picked it up. The name Dallas appeared on the screen with a picture of Diamond and him. I couldn't help but wonder who the hell he was. But instead, I sat her phone back on the nightstand and exited the room.

Walking into the living room my brothers, Duke, Kai, and their two girlfriends, Erica and Shaela, who were sitting on the couch waiting for me.

"How old is that girl?" Erica asked.

She was like my little sister but I didn't appreciate her always trying to be in my business. But, I answered her question anyway.

"She's seventeen."

My brother's mouth dropped in shock.

"Damn, man. She bad and look like a grown woman," Duke said.

"So you niggas just gone fight and be cool like shit ain't never happen?" Erica asked.

"We do all the time."

"KY, you sure you want to do this?" Erica asked.

"It's none of your business," I heard my baby's sweet voice say as she walked into the room with us.

I laughed along with Duke.

"Does your mommy know where you are?" She joked.

Diamond had the meanest scowl on her face and as I looked closer at her, I noticed that she had some gold fangs at the top of her mouth. I thought that shit was dope. I mean, Diamond was bad as hell. Her honey blond hair stopped in the middle of her back and I got lost in her hazel eyes every time I looked into them.

Diamond sitting in my lap snapped me out of my daydream.

"My mother isn't your business, either. I got this, you just worry about yo nigga," Diamond smart mouth ass snapped and I couldn't help but laugh.

"Oh, you think this shit funny? Control her li'l ass before I beat it," Erica warned, causing Diamond to giggle.

"I see someone is mad? But, I'm tired."

"Well, go to bed, little girl. He's busy," Erica said.

I gave Erica that "don't get it fucked up" look because I knew how her mouth could get but they also had no idea how Diamond could get, and I personally couldn't wait to see her crazy side.

"Kyson, can you take me home?"

I shook my head.

She pouted. "I can't sleep if I'm alone."

I stood up and picked her up. "I'll be back in about fifteen minutes," I said as I smirked and carried my baby upstairs while she laid her head on my chest.

I laid with her for twenty-five minutes before she fell asleep. That damn girl did that shit on purpose but I couldn't do shit but laugh. She valued our time together and I liked that shit a lot.

When I decided to head back downstairs, my phone started ringing again.

“Sup?” I answered.

“Sup? Kyson, Kalani misses you,” Meme, my baby mother, said.

I knew she was only calling because she missed this dick.

“I'm busy. Tell Lani daddy will come get her tomorrow,” I said before ending the call.

I felt somebody staring at me so I looked up. I locked eyes with Erica.

“Now you're putting Lani on the back burner for this bitch?”

I took a deep breath and said, “Don't disrespect her, E'. She ain't do shit to you.”

I walked to the door and I was ready for these motherfuckers to be out of my crib. All I wanted to do was to go and make Diamond nut in her sleep. She had no idea the things I was going to teach her. After the crew and I said our goodbyes, I locked everything up and went upstairs.

I undressed and climbed into bed beside her. She must've felt a nigga because she moved back until her back was up against my chest. I wrapped my arms around her and held her until my eyes closed.

The next morning, I awoke to the best feeling in the world. My eyes shot open and Diamond was licking the head of my dick. I couldn't stop the moan that slid out of my mouth.

“Oh, shit!” My toes curled as she deep throated my shit.

She sucked and slurped me for at least fifteen minutes before I shot my seed in her hand. I looked at Diamond, who was eyeing my ten-inch monster. I then grabbed a condom off the nightstand I slid it on and pulled Diamond down.

“You know this is my pussy, right?” I asked as I slapped her ass.

She didn't say a word but she was biting down on her lip.

I guided my dick into her pussy and had the urge to nut. She was my first virgin in a while.

“Ouch! Mmm!” She moaned as I continued to stroke her until all of me was inside of her.

"Damn, ma."

She started bouncing up and down on me and rotating her hips. It felt too good to the point that I couldn't take it much longer. I started pumping at a rapid pace, causing her legs to start shaking.

"Oh... My... God...!" she screamed and I let my seed loose in the condom.

Jumping up, I was about to go flush the condom but when I looked down. The condom had broken.

"What the fuck? Oh hell, no!"

"What?" Diamond asked as she walked passed me, heading towards the shower.

I forgot about the condom breaking and wanted to get up in them guts again. But, I knew I had to tell her. Stepping into the shower behind her, I turned her my way and kissed her lips.

"So, I have something to tell you." She nodded so I continued, "The condom broke."

Her whole face dropped. "What you mean?"

"It means you could get pregnant or not. If so, whatever decision you make I'm one hundred percent behind you."

She shook her head and smiled but said nothing. I didn't know if she was okay or if she might murder my ass. I showered and got out, leaving her standing in the middle of the shower stuck. I changed the sheets on the bed and climbed in before turning on ESPN. As I was watching it, her phone started to ring and it was Keisha.

I dozed off and woke back up and she still wasn't in bed. Getting up, I heard her on the phone.

"I like him, Kee."

I guess Keisha had said some goofy shit because Diamond was laughing hard as hell.

"You just left me alone," I playfully pouted and sat on the couch next to her.

"Yeah that's him," she said before she paused. "Keisha says hey. Okay, bitch bye."

She hung up the phone and climbed onto my lap

"Round two?" she whispered into my ear and started gyrating her hips, causing my dick to get rock hard.

"Come here," I said as I laid her on the couch.

I stepped out of my boxers and climbed between her legs before I slowly entered her and she dug her nails deeper into my back with every inch I fed her.

"Oh, yes, Ky-Kyson!" she moaned.

I started digging deeper and deeper into her guts. I swear if she ever gave my pussy away I'd go crazy.

"Damn D, I'm loving this pussy," I growled into her ear.

Her pussy muscles tightened around my dick and I couldn't pull out so once again, I shot my seed inside of her. We laid on the couch in silence

"I need to go home," she said as she jumped up with her cell phone.

That same nigga Dallas had been blowing her shit up. I got up and walked into the bedroom behind her.

"I thought we could stay in and make love all day," I joked.

Once again, her phone rang.

"Answer it."

She hesitated before finally answering.

"What Dallas?" she said as she then listened to what he had to say.

She shook her head. "I don't love you."

I took the phone from her after she gave me a fearful look. Putting the phone to my ear, this nigga was threatening her life.

"You hear me, Diamond? You belong to Dallas!"

I chuckled into the phone before speaking. "She doesn't belong to you, homie."

"Oh, this must be the nigga whose house she stayed at last night. Bring my girl to her house. I'll be there, waiting."

I hung up and dressed in a San Antonio Spurs throwback jersey, some Levi's blue jeans, and a black Spurs fitted cap that I put on backwards. Diamond dressed in a black romper with some gold sandals and accessorized it with a gold 24k locket chain and some gold hoop earrings. She left her hair in a messy bun and we left.

I decided I would drive my white Bentley.

"This is a nice car. I hope to own one, one day," she said.

I gave her the keys. "It's yours, ma."

She shook her head and laughed. "I can't. It'll make me feel like a hoe."

I was about to laugh until I saw how serious she was. Baby girl was definitely wifey type. She was smart but clueless at the same time.

"Ma, you far from a hoe. Can you drive?"

She nodded so I placed the keys in her hand and told her I'd be right behind her in my 2015 black Cadillac CTS Sedan. After making sure she was buckled, I hopped in my car and drove off. She followed suit and we made our way back to Sunny Clove and turned onto her block. There was a red 2015 Audi sitting in her driveway. I pulled in, she pulled in behind me and we got out at the same time. Her mother and some tall, muscular, bright-skinned nigga with green eyes and tattoos all over his arms, were standing in the doorway.

"Diamond, get your little fast ass in this house!" her mother yelled.

We walked in and I sat down. "Momma, you remember Kyson from last night? This Dallas, my ex."

I threw a nod towards the nigga and hugged her mother. Diamond sat next to me on the couch and looked at Dallas.

"What do you want with me?"

He chuckled. "I told you already when I came back to Compton it was going to be you and me."

Diamond sat back like she was in deep thought so I spoke up. "Look, my man. I don't know what type of shit you on, but Diamond ain't going with you."

I looked over to her and she raised up and kissed my lips. "Thanks, bae. I'm going to go grab some clothes."

Her mother didn't protest and neither did I.

My phone started vibrating in my pocket. Pulling it out of my pocket, Meme named popped up on the screen. I looked around to make sure that Diamond or her momma wasn't sneaking up on a nigga before walking outside to go call her.

"Kyson, where are you?"

I didn't know why she insisted on acting like we were in a relationship. She was just a fuck that went wrong, kind of like me and Diamond's slip up.

"Hello!"

"Yo, I'm with my girl. I'll be there in a minute," I said before hanging up.

I was glad that I drove my car instead of riding with Diamond. I was going to tell her about Lani but at that moment, it wasn't the right time. Walking back towards the house, Diamond was walking out with Keisha in tow but was now dressed in black jeans and a black hoodie with a pair of black Air Maxes. I was confused.

"Where you going, ma?"

"I'm going to your boy's crib. His hoes jumped my bitch so now I'm going to his doorstep."

This girl was a fucking fool. She was not getting involved in that shit. Los fucked with straight hood rats, the kind of hoes that would slice your face and shit. I couldn't have mine out there fighting.

"Nah, go your ass to the crib."

I walked around to my car door and got in but not before rolling down my window and telling her, "I'm not playing."

She shrugged her shoulders and got in her car.

"Good girl," I mumbled before making my way to Meme's crib.

3

DIAMOND

It's been a few days since the Dallas incident and I was back home with my momma. She was barely speaking to me considering her favorite son in law was in town and she just didn't want anybody else for me. I was in the kitchen making some breakfast when she walked in.

"You can't honestly tell me you're going to throw away you and Dallas's relationship for this new nigga?"

I looked at my mom and took a deep breath. The only reason she liked Dallas was because he gave her money to take care of me.

"Yes, I'm willing to throw away everything for Kyson."

She shook her head and gave me a look of disgust. Don't get me wrong, I loved my mother but let's face it, she didn't know shit. Her husband, my father left her after twenty-five years of marriage for his gay assistant.

"I'm not a gold digger. I actually like Kyson." I said as I grabbed my good and proceeded to walk towards by bedroom.

Dallas was starting with us curtesy of my mom.

"Diamond?"

I turned around and faced him, his eyes were red and low.

I shook my head "You smoking again?"

Standing, he walked up to me. "I'm lost without my baby, man."

I was holding back my tears. "It's for the best. Your baby momma and kids need you more than I do."

I couldn't feel sympathy for Dallas. I was moving on because he cheated and got my old best friend Nadia pregnant, twice. That was the moment both our lives changed. I put up with a lot from him, but that was one thing I couldn't take.

I walked into my bedroom and say my plate down. My appetite was ruined. Picking up my phone I called Keisha "Hello." She answered on the first ring.

"I need to get away from my momma house. Dallas is here." I said laying back on my bed.

"I'm on my way."

Five minutes later I heard the horn blow, quickly grabbing my purse and phone. I rushed out of the house without saying a word. She drove a few blocks then pulled into her driveway.

"Where is Kyson?" She asked shutting the engine off and getting out of the car.

"His house."

When we walked into the house her mother was sitting on the sofa watching Jerry Springer "Hey." I spoke and hugged her.

"Hey girl, I see your mother then invited Dallas around there. Be strong don't fall for that shit again."

"Yes. She did and I'm so upset. It's like she's trying to force us together." There was a knock at the front door so I got up to answer it.

Opening the door, Dallas was the last person I expected to be standing here.

"Why are you banging on people's door like that?" I asked.

"Diamond, what's the real reason behind you leaving?" he asked, walking into the living room behind me.

"Nigga, you cheated. I loved yo dumb ass and Nadia was my friend" I said as I tried to fight back my tears, but it was no use because he always made me emotional.

"I know we can get past this."

"I thought we could. I was willing to forgive and fuck with you again but then I found out about Zoe."

I didn't care if I hurt his feelings. Hell, he didn't care about my feelings when he was fucking my best friend. He got up and walked out of the house and I was right behind him.

"Really, you come all the way out here to talk to me and then leave because your bitch ass can't handle the truth?" I yelled. I was clearly pissed and he was laughing.

"Hey, get from in front of my house with that lovey dovey shit!" Keisha's mother snapped.

I looked at Dallas and said, "You have an hour, Dallas. I'll be back," I said before I climbed into the car with Dallas and he took off towards his house.

4

DALLAS

To say a nigga was sad was an understatement. I had a girl and still wanted Diamond. We were perfect for each other, whether she wanted to admit it or not. Nadia blamed me for Diamond cutting her off but it wasn't my fault. Shawty wanted to fuck and me being a young nigga, I fucked her and ended up getting her pregnant. Nadia couldn't wait to tell everybody she was pregnant by me. Even after Diamond beat her ass, she was still trying to push the whole me and her issue. Diamond thought Nadia and I were in a relationship and we weren't. I was just taking care of her and my two seeds. I didn't want her and I didn't know what possessed me to fuck around and get her ass pregnant again.

My phone started ringing, I answered without looking at the Caller ID.

"Dallas, hurry home. The girls and I miss you," Nadia said when I answered.

My mind was on Diamond. I couldn't believe she let this new nigga come in and ruin everything I was going to do to get her back. I finally had her talking to me again and now she had a new nigga.

"I'm on my way, but I'm not alone." I said and hung up before she could respond.

I put the pedal to the floor and flew out of Sunny Clove and headed to my spot out in Los Angeles.

"Why are you with that dude? What do you know about him?"

"I know enough," she said, nonchalantly.

She was always like that. She was not going to sit around and talk about her nigga in a negative way. That was another thing that I loved about her.

"Diamond, do you love me?" I asked and hoped she would say yes. But instead, she shrugged her shoulders.

"Dallas, right now I can't even stand the sight of you."

I felt like shit. But, I needed to talk with her and Nadia so that we could all move past this. I needed her to know that I never meant to hurt her and I still had feelings for her. When we arrived at my house, I stepped out of the car, walked around to her side, and opened the door for her.

"You're such a gentlemen with your cheating ass." she giggled.

I couldn't help but look at her back side. It looked like her hips were spreading. My nose instantly flared, thinking this nigga took the one thing that made her different from these other bitches.

I had to admit, I was still in love with Diamond and I also knew Nadia wasn't about to take this conversation lightly but it was what needed to be said. I was tired of being unhappy just because we had kids together. We weren't married and I had no plans of going back there with her again. I was hoping after this Diamond would see that I was a changed man and take me seriously again.

5

DIAMOND

Getting into the car with Dallas was probably the wrong thing to do. I knew he wasn't going to put me any harm. He was my boyfriend before Kyson and we both needed this closure.. He pulled into his parking garage and we stepped out. I didn't know if he brought me to the house he shared with Nadia. If he did, I was going to beat his ass.

He opened the glass door for me and I stepped on the elevator. It felt awkward being in a closed space and not being able to kiss or hug him. He looked at me and bit down on his lip. I tried my best to ignore his stares.

"Stop looking at me," I laughed.

I was happy when the elevator stopped and we were able to get off. He walked me to the red door and I heard kids playing. My head snapped to the side and I looked at him like he lost his mind.

"Chill, okay?" he asked and I nodded my head.

He pushed the door open and we walked inside. I sat down on the sofa in the living room and watched Savannah and Zoe playing. Dallas walked off toward the balcony and the girls ran up next to me and grabbed my bag. I pulled it back and handed them my Samsung Tablet and phone and they ran off with them.

"Hey, baby," I heard Nadia say.

I stuck my tongue out at the girls, who laughed. She looked around to see who was making her kids laugh and our eyes locked.

"What is she doing here?" she asked as she eyed Dallas.

"We need to talk. I'm going to sit the girls down," he said as he walked into the living and grabbed his daughters.

"Give her, her shit back!" she yelled at the girls and all I could do was laugh.

WHAM!

He backhanded her. I couldn't stand there and watch that.

"It's cool, Dallas. Take them to the back," I said

He did just that and I followed Nadia into the kitchen and sat at the bar. "Would you like something to drink?" she asked, barely making eye contact with me.

"No." I smiled.

"You probably think I'm a fool. I was happy to go and tell everybody Dallas was my baby daddy and now you see how I'm really living," she said with an embarrassed laugh.

"I'm not anyone to judge."

I offered her a smile and Dallas walked into the kitchen.

"Let's talk, shall we?" he said as he sat down next to me.

"What is it, Dallas?"

"You asked me why I fucked Nadia, right? Now, I want to give you both my answer."

I nodded and looked at Nadia, who looked like all the blood had drained from her face.

He continued, "I never wanted to fuck Nadia. I was high and drunk as fuck. Although, that's not an excuse we were going through one of our many break ups and I just needed somebody and Nadia was there, Diamond."

Tears were then rolling down me and Nadia's eyes.

"That's one dumb ass reasons, we always broke up. That one time caused you to fuck my friend?"

I looked at Nadia and said, "What's your reason behind fucking my boyfriend?"

Nadia wiped her eyes and smirked.

"I thought he was sexy and I wanted to fuck him because he kept complaining that you weren't giving it up."

I jumped up and slapped that bitch so hard.

WHAP!

I shouldn't have even been here with this nigga when I had Kyson waiting on me.

"Look, just take me home, I don't have time for this shit." I said as I walked into the living room, grabbed my purse, and headed towards the door and his car.

Ten minutes later, he walked to his car and unlocked the doors. I climbed in and buckled my seatbelt.

When he got in, he handed me my Tablet and cell phone.

"Your baby mommy didn't damage them, did she?" I asked.

"Nah, she knows better. But, you didn't have to slap her," he laughed.

"Yeah, I did."

He started the car and headed back to Keisha's house. When he pulled into the driveway, I jumped out and tried to walk into the house before Dallas could grab me.

"Come here, ma," he said as he pulled me into his embrace.

I felt my heart beating out of my chest. I didn't know what was going on with me but I couldn't be having feelings for Dallas.

"You still love me?"

I nodded. "I'll always have love for you but, this isn't going to happen."

"I will never stop fighting for you."

"Dallas, I'm done. I got the closure I needed now you need to just move on."

I knocked on the door and waited for Keisha to come open it.

"Who is it?" Her loud ass screamed.

"Diamond, girl come bring me to Kyson's."

When we got into the car I broke down "Dallas have you in the feelings."

"He basically out blame on me for him sleeping with Nadia. I'm just so over the shit."

"Fuck him, you got this man who do like you. Don't fuck it up because of Dallas lying ass." Keisha was making sense.

I nodded my head and looked out of the window.

As soon as we walked into the house, Keisha was amazed.

"This house is everything."

I nodded in agreement. I had to admit that Kyson was exactly who they said he was; he was that nigga.

After fixing sandwiches for us and getting us a bottle of water, we went and sat outside.

"Okay now tell me about you and kyson." Keisha said.

"Okay, so our night started off with drama. His two sisters-in-law, Erica and Shaela, were trying to handle me. You know I got crazy on both of them bitches. Not to mention, his brother tried to hit on me, which started a fight between them. We didn't have sex that night, though. But, he did eat my pussy."

Keisha's mouth fell open. "Oh girl, you nasty!" she giggled like a school girl.

Rolling my eyes, I continued, "Well, that morning I woke him up to what I would consider was the best head in the world, from the way he was moaning and curling his toes. He then pulled me on top of him and we fucked for hours."

"Bitch, I'm too happy about this! Oh, Los tells me Kyson has a baby momma?"

My heart dropped. I couldn't believe this shit.

"What the fuck?" I asked.

Keisha must've thought I was about to cry because the next thing I knew, she walked over to comfort me.

"Nah, I'm good. I'm just going to play it cool and see if he tells me the truth."

I stood and walked into the house and Los, Kai, Duke along with those two bitches Shaela and Erica, were in the living room.

"What happened to you?" Los asked, pulling Keisha to the side while I proceeded to sit down.

I grabbed a pre-rolled blunt and lit it, turning the television on. My mind wasn't even on the show. I truly felt something for Kyson, so for him to lie to me was really eating me up and I hoped he told me the truth, soon. I heard the front door open ten minutes later and in walked Kyson, holding the most adorable little baby. She had jet black hair, mocha skin tone like her father, and hazel eyes.

"Diamond, I would like for you to meet my daughter, Lani."

I felt a lump in my throat. I wasn't okay with this.

"Um, she's so beautiful," I smiled and walked out of the front door.

I needed some air so I just took off walking down the road. Before I knew it, my phone started vibrating. Kyson's name flashed across the screen and I answered.

"What's up?"

"Where the fuck you did you go?" a pissed off Kyson asked.

"I'm down the street," I dryly stated.

"Yo ma, wassup? You have a problem with my daughter?"

I took a deep breath, "No, I don't have a problem with her, baby."

"Well, why you leave? Come back."

Turning on my heels, I headed back to the house. I didn't want him to be mad at me.

"Childish ass bitch," Erica snapped.

Without warning, I swung and my fist connected with her jaw.

"Bitch, I'm tired of your old ass trying me."

I felt a pair of hands wrap around my waist and it was Kyson.

"I knew that was coming."

"You're going to let this li'l hoe disrespect your sister?" Shaela retorted and Keisha slapped her ass, too.

"She far from a hoe, bitch!"

I couldn't help but smirk. I bet those hoes were going to think twice before trying me again.

"Come with me," Kyson said as he grabbed my hand and lead me upstairs to a nursery. The room was decorated in pink and yellow birds and butterflies and her crib was solid wood.

Kyson picked her up and handed her to me. "Hold her."

I looked at that nigga like he was crazy. But, that didn't stop him from shoving her into my arms.

"She's so cute," I said as I played with her fingers.

Kyson kissed my cheek. "Meet me in the bedroom in ten minutes."

"You have company, though."

Shrugging his shoulders, he replied, "I don't give a fuck."

I laughed. That nigga was crazy. After handing him the baby, I walked down the hall to his bedroom and quickly undressed. All I had on now was a red lace bra and panties set.

I laid back on the bed and waited for Kyson.

"Damn, you sexy as hell," I heard his deep voice say.

I looked up at him and watched as he undressed. He slowly walked over to me with this sexy face that caused me to giggle.

"What you laughing at?" he asked as he kissed me and laid between my legs.

"Nothing."

I giggled and wrapped my legs around his waist.

"Nah, come ride daddy's tongue," he said and moved to the top of the bed.

Crawling to him, I pulled off my panties and bra and straddled his face.

"Come here Diamond," he said, pulling me onto his tongue.

"Fuck!" I moaned loudly as I grinded my pussy on his tongue.

I had no clue what he was doing to my body but I didn't want it to stop. He slapped my ass and used his thumb to massage my clit while he darted his tongue in and out of me at a rapid pace. My legs started to shake and I couldn't hold it in anymore.

"Oh, my God, baby! Yes, yes, yes!" I screamed not giving a fuck who heard me.

Kyson flipped me over on all fours and rammed his dick inside of me. "

Yes, daddy!"

I started throwing my ass back.

"Fuck, ma. Throw that thing back for daddy!"

He started pounding me harder.

"I'm cumming daddy!"

He started fucking me even harder before he pulled out. He then laid flat on his back and his dick was standing at full attention.

"Come ride yo' shit, ma," he demanded.

I climbed on top of him and guided his dick inside.

"Mmm," I moaned as I worked my pussy just the way he liked.

In just a few days, Kyson had me fucking like a pro.

"Bae, ride this shit!"

I started bouncing up and down on his dick. He gripped my ass and started pumping in and out of me at a fast and rough pace. I knew he was on the verge of nutting so I started tightening my pussy muscles around his dick.

"I'm about to nut, ma! Keep that pussy right there."

He rammed his dick in and out of me, pounding inside of me one last time before he shot his seed into me.

"If you're not pregnant, I'm sure you are now. And, I changed my mind. If you are pregnant, I think we should keep it."

I couldn't help the laugh that escaped my mouth.

"You really are on a roll tonight. First, you think I'm going to accept you lying instead of just telling me the truth about your daughter. And, you said you didn't have kids and now you think I'm going to keep a child that's not wanted?" I laughed, again.

WHAM!

I fell back onto the bed. I was stunned and afraid at the same time.

"Do I look like a joke?" Kyson asked and I shook my head as tears fell from my eyes.

"I'm sorry, ma. Come here."

He climbed into bed and kissed my face.

"I didn't mean to. I don't want to kill a child."

I nodded and laid down. I watched him put his clothes on and exit the bedroom. My phone vibrated and I grabbed it off the nightstand.

It was Keisha informing that she and Los were heading out and that she loved me. I said I loved her too and rolled over to go to sleep.

6

KEISHA

"Bae, get off me," I laughed as Los tickled me.

Los and I had been fucking around for a month now. Diamond nor Kyson knew about us before her birthday.

"Keisha, you should come with me to Atlanta for the rest of the summer."

I quickly shook my head.

"I can't leave Diamond here by herself," I said, honestly.

It's not that I didn't want to go out of town with him, it's just that sometimes we were good and sometimes we were very bad.

"She has Kyson," Los said, trying to convince me, but I wasn't budging.

Something was off about Diamond. She didn't even come down to tell me goodbye and that wasn't like her.

Before I knew it, my phone started ringing. My mother had been blowing my phone up and since I hadn't been home in a few days, I decided to answer.

"Hello."

"Keisha Noelle! Where the fuck are you?" she yelled.

I looked at the phone. I was confused because my mother had

never yelled. In fact, she never cared about where I was or what I was doing.

"I'm with Los."

"You need to come home," he said and without waiting for a response, she hung up.

I was beyond pissed and confused.

"What's going on?"

Getting up from the bed, I grabbed my custom Yeezys that Los bought me for my birthday and put them on.

"She says I need to come home."

Los stood and put on some black Levi's and a white T- shirt with some white Giuseppe Zanotti shoes. I grabbed my black Gucci bag and we headed out the door to his Candy Red Lamborghini. It was crazy how in just a few months, I went from barely eating to eating at the finest restaurants, wearing the best clothes, and even shopping in the best stores. And if my mother thought I was giving that up, she definitely needed to think again.

"What's going on?" Los asked, on edge.

"I don't know," I truthfully stated.

My mind drifted off to the first time my mom made me have sex. I hated that woman with a passion and she didn't even know it. I was thirteen-years-old and my first time was with this drug dealer. He fucked me senseless for her to get a hit. I could remember it like it was yesterday.

"Keisha, get your ass in here!" she yelled from the living room.

I got up from my queen sized bed and sighed. As I walked into the living room, I noticed Pac, a local drug dealer.

"Yes, mother? Hey, Mr. Pac."

"Mommy needs a hit."

I shrugged my shoulders. I was confused.

"This man is going to take you into your bedroom and do whatever he wants to you," she said.

"But, why?" I asked as tears formed in the corner of my eyes

WHAM!

"I don't ask you for shit. I take care of your black ass, don't I? Now, get in that room."

I turned and ran to my bedroom. Before I could shut the door, Pac was standing in the doorway with his hands up. He walked in and shut the door. My heart was beating fast. I mean, I had a mini crush on Pac but this was crazy.

"I don't want to hurt you, girl," he said, sitting down on the bed and taking his jacket off.

His black .9mm pistol was displayed on his waist. He caught me looking at it and removed it to sit it on my dresser.

"Why are you here?" I asked above a whisper.

"I want you."

He moved closer to me and I tried moving away but it was to no avail. He pulled me under him and got in between my young thighs.

"Please stop!" I yelled as he unbuckled my shorts and pulled them off along with my panties.

He stood and took off his clothes and his dick was huge.

I knew for a fact he wasn't putting that inside of me.

"Keisha, come over here," he said as he sat on the bed.

Still, I didn't move.

"I guess I have to come to you," he sighed, walked up to me, and grabbed a fist full of my hair before he pushed me to my knees.

"Open up!" he stated with cold eyes.

When he saw that I wasn't cooperating, he grabbed his gun and pressed it against my head.

"Open the fuck up!"

I opened my mouth as tears fell from my eyes. I felt something enter my mouth and pushed to the back of my mouth, causing me to gag so much so that I started coughing violently. He then pulled me up, laid me on the bed, and positioned himself between my legs. Before I could protest or put up a fight, he rammed his dick inside of me.

"Ahhhh!" I screamed as he then placed his hand over my mouth to muffle my cries.

"Please, stop! Stop!" I screamed, hoping my mom would come in. But, the bitch never did.

~

"Keisha! Keisha!" I heard Los yelling as he shook me.

"Damn, don't kill me," I laughed as I opened my eyes and looked into his coal, black eyes.

This man held no emotion, no compassion, and no mercy for others. I had no idea why he was so sweet to me and in the streets, people feared him and Kyson left and right.

"We're here," I said as we walked into my mother's house.

I looked at my mother, Sherlene, who was standing in the living room of our three bedroom, two bath brownstone.

"Wassup, mom?" I asked as I took a seat on our leather couch.

"I'm going to rehab and I'm signing your emancipation forms. I thought about it and I know that I never did shit for you and I sold you for drugs."

Los looked at me and I put my head down. I was embarrassed that she would say that.

"Okay, momma."

"Okay? I'm telling your little ungrateful ass that you can stay in this house and do you."

"Me? Ungrateful? Really, mom?"

I stood and made my way to the front door. As I pulled it opened, two officers and her probation officer were at the door so she ran and signed the papers.

"I won't let the system get my daughter," she said as she handed me the papers and peacefully walked out with the officers.

"Yes!" I screamed jumping up and down.

I was finally free from that bitch.

"We need to talk," he said.

I settled down and sat back on the couch. I knew what was

coming since my mother just let one of my deepest, darkest secrets out. Diamond didn't even know about this.

"What happened?" he asked as he pulled me onto his lap.

"Um, I was thirteen when it happened. The guy was a local drug dealer that I knew from around the way."

Los didn't say anything so I continued, "Well, my mother needed a hit."

I stopped and bit my bottom lip, "But, she was broke, I guess, so she came home with the guy."

I broke down into tears.

"I was just a little girl, Los. I had no idea what I was doing." I cleared my throat. "She called me into the living room to tell me that that guy was going to do whatever he wanted to me."

Los shook his head in disgust "He raped me for five hours."

Tears started to flow once again and Los pulled me into his arms.

"I'm not leaving you down here like this."

I chuckled. "I told you I'd talk to Diamond whenever I go by there."

"I heard you. Now, give me a tour."

Los stood and pulled me up with him.

"Well, this is the living room," I said as we walked through the double doors. "The kitchen and that's the den."

We then walked upstairs and into my mother's old room.

"This will be my room as soon as I get all of her stuff out of here, there's the guest room, and this is my room," I said as I twisted the knob to the bedroom that held every secret, every sin, and every prayer.

My bedroom was decorated in pink cheetah colors. The bed sat in the middle of my room and I had a walk-in closet that was filled with clothes and shoes. One thing I had to admit about Pac was that after that incident, he'd been taking good care of me.

Los walked over to my dresser and picked up a picture of my daddy, Dave "Big D" Cruz.

"Big D was your father?"

I nodded.

"Wow, he put Kyson and me on. I looked up to him like a father," he said.

I sat down and smiled, thinking about my father. I wish he was here now. But, unfortunately, he died.

Los sat down on the bed and I climbed on top of him. I wasted no time kissing him.

"Damn, you miss the dick?"

Nodding, I pulled his nine-inch dick from his pants and placed it into my mouth.

"Oh shit," he moaned and I bobbed my head up and down.

He grabbed a fist full of my hair and started pumping in and out of my mouth until his seed hit the back of my throat. He pulled me up and laid me back. He took my clothes off before he flicked his tongue over my clit and softly pinched my nipples.

"Ahhhh!" I moaned out.

"Cum for me!" he said putting his mouth on my clit, flicking his tongue at a rapid pace.

My legs started to shake and I arched my back. "I'm cumin!" I moaned as I viciously humped his face.

I watched him stand up and place a condom on his erect penis and laid back on the bed.

He flipped me over and slowly inserted his dick in from the back, causing my back to arch.

"Yeah, right there!" he groaned as he pounded away at my guts.

"Fuck! Shit! Oh...God," I couldn't even formulate a whole sentence because he was dicking me down so good.

After a few more strokes, he filled the condom up with his seeds and went to flush it.

I heard my phone vibrating so I grabbed it out of my bag. Diamonds name popped up on the screen.

"Hey, girl," I answered on the first ring.

"Hey, hoe, are you ready?."

"Yea, Los is going to drop me off over there."

"Okay, I'll be waiting."

I hung up the phone and went into the restroom to take a quick shower. I got out and dressed in a long maxi dress with some black and Gold sandals. My hair was in a ponytail. Los was laying in the middle of the bed with his eyes closed. "Drop me off at Kyson's."

He nodded "I need to go holla at my nigga anyway."

We walked out of the house and to his red BMW.

"Where y'all going?" He asked starting the car and heading towards Kyson's side.

Nail and hair salon," I said as I put on some nude lip gloss.

It was a good thing that Kyson didn't stay too far from me. Before we knew it, we were pulling up to his garage.

"Oh, good my nigga here," Los said as he killed the ignition.

We got out and walked to the front door. After knocking a hundred times, Kyson finally opened the door.

"She's still in the bed," he lied.

I almost cursed his ass out until I saw Diamond walking downstairs, dressed in a beige maxi dress and some Jimmy Choo sandals.

My bitch was bad as hell and if a bitch tried to say she wasn't, that hoe was hating.

"Hey Keisha," she hugged me and kissed Kyson on the lips and I did the same to Los as we left the house.

7

DIAMOND

Waking up this morning, my face was killing me. I got up and went into the bathroom I had a black eye. After brushing my teeth and trying to cover up the bruise with makeup. I exited the restroom. I was not trying to be in the house all day looking at him and Lani.

Kyson stepped out of bed and went into the restroom.

“Good morning, beautiful,” he said Trying to kiss me but I turned my head to the side.

He was dressed in a black T-shirt, some blue jean Levi’s, and red Giuseppe Zanotti sneakers. He brushed his hair and pulled on a black Chicago Bulls fitted cap and walked across the hall to get Lani dressed. I had no idea where they were going.

“Baby, we out!” I heard Kyson yell from the stairs. I rushed behind them.

I was disgusted. If he thought that after putting his hands on me that everything was okay, it wasn't. “I doubt I’ll be here when y'all get back,” I spoke nonchalantly.

He didn't say anything just nodded his head and walked out of the house. I was right behind him. I got into the Bentley with Keisha and took off towards Zyria’s Hair and Nail Salon.

"How was your night?" she asked.

I removed my shades and looked at her.

"Oh my God, D.! What the hell happened?"

"Honestly, I don't remember. I don't know if he hit me because I beat Erica's ass or because he felt like I disrespected his daughter."

"Are you leaving him?"

Looking out the rearview mirror, I shook my head.

"No, I'm not leaving him. Would you leave Los?"

"No."

"Okay then," I said as I parked the car and climbed out.

The shop was busy when we stepped in.

"You can tell it's the weekend," Keisha laughed as she sat next to me.

I only nodded. Erica was walking into the shop with Shaela and another chick.

"She would be in here."

"Zy, how long before I get in the chair?" I asked my stylist as I walked over to Zyria's private room.

Before she could answer, we heard something fall.

"Bitch, I'll punch you in yo' mouth," I heard Keisha say and before I could make it to her, she punched Shaela in the mouth.

"Oh, hell no!" Zyria yelled as she tried to help me pull Keisha off Shaela.

Erica just stood her scary ass off to the side.

"Diamond!" I heard Kyson say.

"You fighting again?" he asked as he grabbed my hand and pulled me outside.

"No, I was breaking it up. Why you even here?"

He nodded "I missed you."

My face twisted up in confusion. This nigga was bipolar.

"Uh, ok."

"She's with her Godmother."

I half smiled.

"You want to roll with me to get her?"

I shook my head.

"And miss my hair appointment? No, sir."

"We're not getting her until later. I want to spend some time with you."

I loved the gesture but, wasn't too much feeling him at the moment " Keisha was already getting her nails done.

"I'm ready, D," Zyria said as she washed her hands.

Sitting in the chair, I laid my head back.

"Those shades have to go," Zyria laughed.

Chuckling, I removed them and sat back. Zyria's smile was quickly replaced with a look of concern and sympathy. I shut my eyes and enjoyed my shampoo and wash. I turned my phone on loud and played to Tink's song, "*Treat Me Like Somebody*".

When she was done washing my hair, she sat me under the dryer and that's when Dallas texted me. He'd been blowing me up all day. It was his birthday and I didn't text him on purpose. Shit, he didn't tell me Happy Birthday. After telling me that he missed me and asking me to come to his party later, I told him no and just stopped texting him. I was going to bring it to Kyson's attention, though.

"Who are you texting?" Keisha asked as she sat next to me.

"Dallas."

"That black eye not gone stop you, huh?" she asked just as Zyria walked over and pulled me from under the dryer.

"How do you want it?"

"A wrap," I said as I watched a chick with two kids walk in. She was bad to the bone.

"Hey, I have an appointment with Zyria," she said then turned and started walking toward us.

"Tatiyana? Long time no see. Look at Addison and Sawyer. They are so big," Zyria said.

"Girl, they grown as fuck, too," Tatiyana spoke, looking down at me and playing with her daughter's hair.

"Tati? What are you doing out here?" Erica asked.

"I need my hair done and so do these two," she answered, rolling her eyes.

"Have you heard from Kyson?" Erica asked, looking directly at me.

I looked at Keisha to make sure she caught the shade, too.

"Ugh, no. I have no interest in him," she said as she twisted up her mouth.

I couldn't help but look at her. She was beautiful. Her flawless, almost white skin tone, jet-black hair, and green eyes almost left me speechless.

"Diamond, this is Tatiyana. Tatiyana this is Diamond, Kyson's new girlfriend since E. trying to be messy," Zyria said.

"Um, hello. You and your daughters are gorgeous," I said to Tatiyana just as Kyson and Los were walking in along with Duke and Kai.

"Hey bae," Kyson said.

"Hey, baby, what you doing here?" I asked, looking at Kyson who was looking at Tatiyana.

"Tatiyana? Wassup, ma?" he said as she chuckled.

"What's up, Kyson," she said, turning to Zyria. "How much longer?"

"Well, I have one ahead of y'all."

She sighed. "Well, girls, do you want to go shopping on daddy."

"Yeah!" the two girls yelled while standing. They were dressed in yellow and white sundresses and they wore custom Chanel sandals. Both of their hair was in French braids that stopped in the middle of their backs.

I didn't know what to think at this point but, I sure as hell was going to get to the bottom of this shit.

"It was nice meeting you, Diamond," Tatiyana said, snapping me out of my thoughts.

"Likewise," I said, raising my eyebrows.

Turning around, I assumed she gave Kyson a look because he followed her outside.

"That's your man following that pretty ass girl out of here?" a gay male hairstylist named Pink asked.

I guess it surprised them that I didn't get out of my seat to run after them.

"That's his daughter's Godmother. What they had or didn't have isn't my business," I said, looking at Erica and Shaela before putting my shades back on and my headphones back into my ears.

8

ERICA

These little ass girls who were now in our circle were doing way too much for me. Kyson was already hitting on his little girlfriend and just like the fool I thought she was, she was letting him. He was tagging that ass from the looks of that eye.

"What are we doing tonight?" I asked Shaela.

She looked at Diamond and asked, "Do you want to come to a birthday party with us tonight?"

I couldn't believe that shit. I wasn't trying to be babysitting all fucking night. Even though I had a nigga, I wasn't going to be sitting on the sidelines because Diamond nigga was controlling.

"Um, sure. I wouldn't mind," she said, looking over at Kyson who shrugged his shoulders and eyed both Shaela and me.

"Keisha, you too?" I said, looking at her. She mugged me then laughed along with Diamond.

I was already annoyed with these two hoes. I pulled Shaela to the side and hit her upside the head with my hand.

"What the fuck?" she asked, pushing me.

"Why would you invite Diamond to the party tonight?"

She cocked her head to the side and put her hands on her hips.

"Why would you invite Keisha?"

I shook my head. "Because you invited her and I don't have anything against Keisha."

"Okay and I don't have anything against Diamond," she said and sat down at the table so she could get her feet done.

"Well, I hope y'all have a good time," I stated and walked off.

Heading over to where Keisha was, I took a seat in a chair and the gay hair stylist twirled me around.

"So, what are you two wearing to the party?" I asked as the guy washed my hair.

"I'm not sure yet. But, I'm going to shut it down," I heard Diamond say to Keisha, Zyria, and Shaela.

I shook my head and laughed. She reminded me of Tatiyana too much.

An hour later when my hair was finished, we were on our way to the mall with Keisha and Diamond behind us in Kyson's two-door white Bentley.

"I've always wanted to drive that car and Kyson would never let me drive it. But, she comes along and he just hands her the keys like it's nothing," I said as I eyed Shaela, who was too busy texting on her phone to hear anything I said.

"Did you hear me?" I tapped her on the leg.

"Hmm? Yeah, I heard you but I'm not talking about Diamond with you. I actually think she's cool people."

I frowned and stuck my tongue out at her.

"What are you wearing tonight?"

Shaela looked at me and twisted her nose up. "Bitch, am I not on my way to the mall with you?"

I couldn't help but laugh. "I was just asking. I really need an idea for my outfit but I think I want to wear a high waisted skirt, crop top, and some wedges."

When we arrived, I pulled up, parked next to Diamond and climbed out.

"Erica, you look good today," Keisha said.

I was dressed in a black maxi dress and Prada flip flops. People thought I looked like Nicki Minaj, but I didn't have her ass. I laughed to myself and walked through the mall beside of Keisha and Shaela. Diamond kept her distance and I couldn't help but smirk. I really didn't have a reason not to like the girl, I just didn't want her with Kyson. He deserved someone that he could see himself marrying and I just didn't see that in Diamond. She was clueless and didn't know shit about him.

"Erica, what's your beef with my bitch?" Keisha asked as we walked around the Chanel store.

"I don't have beef with her. She's the one who hit me."

"Well, you provoked her."

"Look, I understand that's your friend and everything and you're both new to the circle but your friend doesn't belong with my brother."

Keisha was looking dumbfounded. Diamond stepped in front of us and said, "Look, I heard what you said. I think it's crazy that you don't think I'm good enough for your brother because I am. And, I really like him. Nothing you or anybody else say is going to change how we feel about each other."

I half believed her. "I've seen him give his heart to some girls who just shitted on him in the end."

"I'm not here to hurt him," Diamond said, genuinely.

"Oh, Erica I found the perfect outfit for you! Come here," Shaela yelled, breaking the awkwardness.

I stepped into the dressing room with her and tried on a nude Zebina bandage dress.

"I love it and I know what shoes I want to wear with it."

I was so happy. Tonight, I was looking for a side nigga and Dallas was on my list.

He was fine, paid, and a boss. I needed him on my team. The rest of the girls got their outfits and Diamond was the only one being secretive about what she was wearing. I couldn't wait to get home and get some shut-eye. A bitch was mad tired. After dropping Shaela off to her and Kai's crib, I made my way home.

Pulling up to the house, Duke car was in the driveway.

"Hey baby," Duke greeted me with a kiss on a cheek.

"Hey, where are the boys?" I asked, referring to our twin sons, Duke Jr and Dyer.

"Upstairs. Where you headed to tonight?" he asked with an attitude like he had every night I went out.

"Out with Shaela, Keisha, and Diamond."

Kyson looked at me and shook his head. "Y'all really welcoming my girl and not just trying to get her out to fuck with her, right?"

I shrugged my shoulders.

"I'm surprised you letting her go and don't know what you're talking about. She hit me remember?" I said, making my way the master bedroom.

I laid on the bed and closed my eyes.

Before I knew it, I jumped up, looked at the clock on my phone and almost screamed. The party started at ten o'clock and it was already going on twelve. I had ten missed calls from Shaela and Keisha.

"Oh shit!" I yelled and made my way to the shower and jumped in.

I quickly bathed and lotioned up with Cocoa Butter. After throwing on my dress, I slipped my feet into some nude Christian Louboutins. After grabbing my Gucci clutch, I walked out of the house.

9

NADIA

I was starting to wonder if Dallas and I would ever get back to the way things were at first. We were getting ready for Dallas's birthday party at club Larue in Long Beach. He was turning twenty-five and didn't act like it.

"Nadia, there's no leaving early," he said, I figured he was trying to get me not to go since he invited Diamond.

"Okay, Dallas."

I stepped into my Matisse bandage two-piece dress and Cross Index Velvet 'N Chain heels. My hair was styled into loose curls that stopped in the middle of my back.

"You look nice," I said, admiring Dallas.

He was dressed in all white wearing a polo button-down, Girbaud jeans, and Air Force Ones.

"Thanks. You look good, too."

He kissed my forehead and we walked downstairs and out of the house. When we arrived at the club, it was packed.

"Ugh, do you even know any of these people?" I asked.

"Does it matter? I'm just looking to have a good time for my birthday."

He mean-mugged me. I was trying not to get on his nerves so I kept my mouth shut. As soon as we stepped out of the black and gold 2015 Rolls Royce, the crowd went crazy.

"That's him!" I heard a girl yell.

I intertwined my hand with his and we made our way into the club.

There were people walking up from everywhere hugging him and telling him Happy Birthday. People I had never even seen him hold a conversation with.

"Hey, birthday boy," I heard a familiar voice say as she hugged him like I wasn't even standing there.

"Diamond, wassup, ma? I'm glad you could make it."

Dallas was smiling and showing all thirty-two teeth and pissing me the hell off. I knew he still loved Diamond. Hell, he never let me forget that shit. But, I wasn't playing the background. At least not tonight. This was my man's birthday party and I planned on being on his arm all night.

"Hey Diamond," I spoke and she gave me this smug look like she was better than me.

"Nadia," she smiled and walked off with her girls.

I walked away from Dallas because I needed a drink.

"What can I get you?" the bartender asked.

"Vodka."

"You sure about that?" someone from behind me asked.

I turned around and was face-to-face with Seven. He was a friend of Dallas's that I met a few years ago at a barbecue Brenda was throwing.

"Seven? Hey," I said and watched him scan the room.

He always made sure he was safe and had his piece on him before relaxing. He didn't trust anybody.

"Damn, she bad."

I followed his eyes as they fell upon Diamond. I had to admit that she was gorgeous.

"That's Diamond."

"Wait? The Diamond? The one Dallas and Kyson are in love with?"

I nodded and didn't take my eyes off her.

"Damn, I'll be right back."

I slouched in my chair. On the low, I had a thing for Seven. But, I wouldn't dare tell him. I tried coming on to him once and he shut that shit down with the quickness. His loyalty to Dallas ran deep and I had to respect that.

I watched as he disappeared into the crowd. Turning around, I knocked my shots back before standing and making my way to the VIP area. I felt like starting some shit and if I had to start with Diamond, then so be it. The VIP area wasn't too crowded considering everyone was down on the dance floor trying to show off.

"You good?" Kyson's fine ass asked and I couldn't help but blush.

"Yes, I'm good. Thank you."

I looked on the dance floor and watched as Diamond was swaying her hips back and forth. My face frowned up as I watched Dallas wrap his arms around Diamond's waist, trying to dance with her.

Kyson witnessed the whole thing, too. He turned around and had a whole mug on his face. He stormed out of the VIP area and made his way downstairs. I laughed. I was going to enjoy the rest of my night whether Dallas was with me or not. I was tired of his shit. Like him not coming home at night and the fact that he made me cut off all my friends, including Diamond.

For the rest of the night, I sat in VIP and got drunk until Dallas approached me.

"Go home," he said as he threw some money on the bar and walked off.

I knew he was mad and I really didn't give a fuck. I politely got up and walked out of the club without saying a word to anybody.

"Your cab is here," the bouncer said.

"Cab? Where's Dallas?"

"He's still here."

I couldn't understand what he was trying to do.

"Okay."

I turned around and tried to get back into the club but the bouncer stopped me. "Nah, ma. He said go home."

I started to cry. I got into the cab, pulled out my cell phone, and shot him a text.

Me: *I'm leaving yo' ass.*

Baby: *Okay, just make sure you leave my kids.*

I didn't even have it in me to respond. I was done with him treating me like shit. Once I made it to the crib, I paid the cab driver, got out, and made my way to the condo we purchased. I walked into the house and immediately broke down.

"This cannot be happening to me," I mumbled.

I cried until all I could do was lay on the floor in the living room and go to sleep.

10

DIAMOND

The whole club scene was new to me. I couldn't believe Kyson let me come to Dallas's party. Well, he didn't know it was actually Dallas's party.

"D, damn you wearing the hell out of that dress," Keisha complimented me.

I looked down to admire my Stefina studded two-piece dress and Mona sandals.

"Diamond, you slaying mama," my home girl, Candice, said as all the ladies with her looked me up and down and gave me an approving nod. I was finally was able to cover up my bruise with makeup and it looked natural.

"Your man just stepped in the spot," Keisha said as I looked towards the front entrance to see Dallas walking in with Nadia on his arm.

Keisha, Shaela, and I made our way over to them and as soon as I spoke, Dallas dropped Nadia's hand.

"Hey birthday boy," I greeted him with a hug.

"Diamond, wassup ma? Glad you could make it."

Dallas's eyes roamed over my body. He really thought he had a chance but in reality, he didn't. Looking at Nadia I knew I wasn't going to speak so I just gave her the meanest mug I could muster.

"Oh, shit. Your real man just stepped into the building," Keisha said and pulled me away from Dallas before Kyson could see us.

Walking over to them, I heard the chick say "I miss you."

"Oh, do you? Or do you miss this dick?" I heard him say as he spun her around.

"Wow!"

That was the only thing I could say as tears trickled down my cheek.

"Diamond, come here ma," he said and like the fool I went.

"Why are you here?" he asked.

"This was the party Shaela and Erica were talking about."

We walked out of the club. Heading to the car, we saw Tatiyana walking up with two other girls that looked Identical to her.

"Hey Diamond," she spoke and I smiled.

"Hey, Tatiyana."

"You leaving already?"

I looked at Kyson, who looked at me and shook his head. "Nah, I just need to holla at her real quick."

They passed us and he kissed my neck.

"Let me get some." I couldn't help but laugh at him.

"Boy, we can't fuck out here."

"Why not?" he asked, pulling me towards his 2014 black Tahoe and opening the door.

He pushed me into the backseat and shut the door.

"Come here, ma," he said and I climbed on top of him, pulling off my dress.

"Damn, you sexy as fuck ma. And, keep the heels on."

He pushed me back, slid my panties to the side, and flicked his tongue back and forth on my clit.

"Ahh!" I screamed out as he latched on to my clit and sucked on it.

After ten more minutes, both our phones started vibrating. We ignored them. Lying back, he pulled his dick out. I took him into my mouth and sucked until it got hard.

"Ride your shit, ma," he demanded and I climbed on top of him and slowly slid down his pipe.

"Mmm," I moaned as he rocked my hips back and forth.

We went at it like that for a few minutes until he flipped me over and rammed his dick back into me.

"Fuck!" he groaned in my ear as he slapped my ass and pumped in and out at a rapid pace. "I'm cumming, ma!"

After he came we cleaned ourselves up and exited the car. When I finally looked at my phone, I had a text message from Dallas telling me to come to the VIP section.

We walked back into the club and Kyson and I went our separate ways, but not before he kissed me.

"See you later, you riding with me?"

I nodded my head and walked straight to VIP. Dallas was sitting at a round table with his friends surrounding him.

"Sorry about that," I whispered in his ear and he turned around and smirked.

"Let me find out you giving my pussy away?" he spat as his friends and Nadia watched us.

"Dallas, don't make a scene," I said and walked away from him, towards the girls.

"You know him?" Erica asked.

"Yeah, that's my ex."

I laughed at the sound of that and so did Keisha.

"Y'all have history?"

I sat down, grabbed a shot and downed it. The liquor instantly had my throat burning.

"Yeah, we have history. But, enough about his punk ass."

I laughed as I stood up and took another shot. I wanted to let loose and have fun. Keisha and I went down to the dance floor and started dancing. I felt somebody watching me so I looked back at the bar. Kyson and Los sat with their eyes locked on us. I smiled at him and returned dancing.

"Here," Keisha said, handing me another shot. I knocked it back.

I felt a pair of hands wrap around my waist and they weren't Kyson's. Looking back, I almost had a heart attack.

"Dallas, move!" I yelled trying to pry his hands off me.

"Uh, oh! Here comes Kyson," Keisha said.

I was still trying to get Dallas's hands from around my waist. But, before I knew it, he hit Dallas in the face with the butt of his gun, knocking him unconscious almost immediately.

He grabbed my hand and yanked my ass out of the club so fast. Without warning, I felt his hand across my face.

WHAP! WHAP!

I screamed out in pain, holding my face. We had a few onlookers but no one said anything.

"Go get in the car!" he yelled.

I ran towards the car and climbed in. He just had to act a fool tonight. I thought. My phone vibrated letting me know I received a text.

Best friend: *He told me to take your car home, you alright?*

Me: *I'm cool. Tell Shaela and Erica I had a good time*

Best friend: *okay, I got you ma. I love you.*

Me: *love you too*

Kyson got into the car, started it, and made his way to the house. Once we got home, he wasted no time pinning me against the wall.

"You thought that shit was cute?"

I couldn't even answer because his hands were wrapped around my throat but I shook my head.

"What? Open your mouth, Diamond!" he screamed as he released the tight grip he had on me.

I dropped to the floor and gasped for air.

"Get the fuck up!" he said as he yanked me up and dragged me up the stairs.

When we got into the room, he threw me on the floor and stepped over me but not before kicking me in the ribs.

"Please, stop!" I mumbled, barely able to breathe.

"Oh stop! That's what you want," he said as he continued to kick me. "I can't even look at you!"

He stood and walked out of the room.

Standing, I limped into the restroom.

"Ah!" I winced in pain and sat down on the toilet, allowing the tears to flow. I stood up after five minutes of crying my eyes out and turned on the shower. I stepped in and stood under the water. I was ready to go home. I needed a break from Kyson and everything else so I called my brother and with no hesitation, he came and picked me up. I left without letting Kyson know.

Three months later....

Kyson been blowing my phone up consistently and now that he learned I am indeed pregnant with his seed, he had been doing any and everything he could to try to get to me, including making Shaela and Erica cut me off. I didn't care because I was over his dumb ass hitting me. Even though Kyson pistol whipped him, it was never about Kyson. We had a friendship before dating. Just thinking about Dallas made me send him a text message.

Me: *Hey, I miss you dude*

Dallas: *Nah baby, I miss you*

Me: *How much?*

Dallas: *Too much, I'ma show you how much*

When I spotted Keisha pulling up, I put my phone away.

"Diamond, Kyson is really worried about you," she started as soon as I got in the car with her.

"Thanks for picking me up. This baby got me lazy."

"Girl anything for my sister and god baby."

All I could do was smile. This fucking baby had me throwing up all the time and nauseous. I was ready to get this shit over with. My phone rang and Kyson's named popped up on the screen.

"Answer it, please," Keisha pleaded, causing me to finally gave in.

"Hello," I answered with a attitude.

I had to admit I missed him but I wasn't feeling the ass whoopings.

"Come home, ma," Kyson said and I chuckled.

"I don't know."

I was really clueless. He started promising that he wouldn't hit me again and that I was the only girl he needed in his life along with our child. I believed him and went home. My heart was racing as we turned on his street and I noticed Los's car in the driveway. Keisha sucked her teeth and rolled her eyes.

"What's been going on?" I asked with my eyebrows raised in confusion.

"Girl, he's been trying to beat me for any and everything."

I couldn't do shit but shake my head.

"Honestly, I'm afraid of what Kyson is going to do to me for just leaving him in the middle of the night."

Keisha looked at me shocked but didn't say anything.

Getting out of the car, We walked up to the door. Keisha pushed it open and made our way into the house.

"Aye, wassup baby?" I heard Los yell as I walked into the living room behind her.

Kyson almost ran up to me.

"Baby, you're big!" Erica blurted out, causing everyone to laugh as well as Kyson.

"Bae, I missed you," he said as he hugged and kissed me.

I couldn't believe I was seventeen and pregnant for a man I was in love with and scared as hell of.

"I um, m-mi-missed you, too," I stammered.

I needed to sit down and that's just what I was planning to do as I grabbed a chair from the table and say in it.

"Are you going to talk to me?"

I ignored him.

"I left because I shouldn't be getting hit on."

He placed his hand on my stomach but didn't say anything. Then, he stood up and punched me.

WHAM!

He punched me dead in the mouth.

"Shut the fuck up! Since you want to leave without telling me, I'm going to show you something," he yelled as he continued to beat me.

The pain I felt was unbearable. A million thoughts were running through my head.

"Don't leave out of this room!" Kyson demanded before marching out of the bedroom.

I got up and went to go take a shower before getting back into bed. I was probably dumb as hell for staying but I'd be damned if this nigga killed me and my baby. I couldn't move. I winced in pain and then heard a gushing sound and my pants were soaked. I was about to walk out of the room when Shaela walked in.

11

SHAELA

I couldn't believe my ears as I listened to Kyson beat on Diamond. Her screams and cries for help were faint and that worried me, so I hid in the restroom until I heard their bedroom door shut and made my way to the door. I slowly opened it and Diamond was in the bed sleeping.

"Shhh."

Her eyes popped open and she tried to hide her face from me.

"Stop, don't hide from me."

I went through the same thing with Kai. It ran in their family. Those pussy ass niggas couldn't keep their hands to themselves for shit. They learned from the best, considering their pops used to beat the fuck out of their mother.

She shook her head and winced in pain.

"Are you okay?" I asked and she shook her head.

"No, I think I need to go to the hospital."

My heart truly went out to this girl. I mean, I went through shit with Kai whooping my ass. Sometimes when he felt like he was in the wrong, he found a way to blame me and beat me for that.

"Why did you come back?"

"He made promises. Look, can you get me to the hospital?" she asked. I stood and walked out of the room.

Five minutes later, I was came back into the room with Keisha who picked her up and walked out of the house with her. We sat her in the front seat of my Tahoe and pulled off, heading towards the hospital. They quickly rushed Diamond to the back so we just sat in the waiting room. Her mother and another dude walked in fifteen minutes later.

"Keisha!" a woman who looked similar to Diamond called out.

"Mrs. Carter? Hey," Keisha said as she hugged her.

"What happened?" Dallas asked.

"What you know about that cat?" Los asked, nudging me in the arm and throwing his head towards Dallas.

"What the fuck happened? She was okay before going upstairs with Kyson's ass!" Erica said as she sat next to me.

"Kyson whooped her ass. I heard the whole altercation. When I went in to check on her, that's when she told me she needed to go to the hospital," I said, my mind racing.

"I wonder what the fuck she said to him to make him snap."

Erica was slowly but surely pissing me off.

"She didn't say anything to him. That nigga just whooped her ass," I spat as I stood and walked away from her.

"Why do you always jump to her rescue when I say something about her?" she asked, standing in front me.

"I'm jumping to her rescue because she isn't here to defend herself. I'm telling you from what I heard. She didn't say anything to him. For you to think she did something to him for him to beat on her is blowing my fucking mind."

I walked back over to my seat just as Kyson was walking from the back.

"Is she okay?" Keisha and Mrs. Carter asked at the same time.

He cleared his throat. "She had the baby."

He spoke with his head down and I felt so bad for Diamond.

"Can we go see her?" I asked as I mean-mugged him.

Kai was looking at me with confusion. Kyson nodded and walked out of the waiting room. I made my way to the back along with Keisha and her mother. As we neared the door, I heard Diamond crying. My heart broke when we entered the room and she was holding a baby boy who was no bigger than her hand.

"I'm so sorry," I said, hugging her. She cried in my arms before Keisha grabbed her and they cried together.

I needed to get out of this hospital before I killed Kyson. He was the reason his girl lost her baby and was out there acting like he wasn't.

"Aye Shaela, how is she?" Los asked.

I looked at all the niggas before my eyes landed on Kyson.

"She's shattered. Her heart is broken and her only purposed for living isn't with her anymore. How would you feel?" I asked before walking out of the hospital with Kai right behind me.

I was done with Kyson after tonight.

Kyson

It was Diamond's and my first anniversary and I couldn't have been happier. I'd been cool and hadn't put my hands on her after she lost our baby boy. I had changed my ways, although it was too late for our child.

"Diamond, ma, you are beautiful," I beamed, looking at my girl who was dressed in a long black dress with some Christian Louboutin heels. Her hair was pulled back into a high bun and she accessorized it with 10 karat princess cut diamond and white gold earrings and a Certified Solitaire pendant that was 18k white gold.

"Baby, you look good yourself," she said.

I walked towards her and kissed her lips. She slid her tongue into my mouth and I gladly opened for her. Pinning her against the wall, I lifted her dress up, unbuckled my belt and slid my pants down. This was our party and if she wanted some dick I didn't care where it was I was giving it to her.

"Hold on baby, let me take this dress off," Diamond said as she panted.

Lately, we'd been going at it all the time. She had become my right-hand man. She sat in on meetings, but that was only because I needed to know she could take care of home if a nigga ever got knocked. When her dress was off, she laid on the bed with her legs up in the air, waiting for me.

I walked over to her, pulling my boxers off along with my pants and entered her slowly.

"Mmm, Kyson," she moaned in my ear as she dug her nails deep into my back.

"Fuck, baby," I groaned.

She was wet as fuck and her pussy was super tight. I didn't know how long I was going to last in the pussy so I decided to make it worth it. I flipped her ass over and pulled her off the bed.

"Touch your toes," I demanded. She did just that and looked back at me, biting her bottom lip. That made me rock hard.

I re-entered her and started hitting her with some long deep strokes.

"Fuck!" she screamed as I held her in place and beat her back out.

Thirty minutes later, someone was beating on our bedroom door and yelling for us to come out, with our nasty asses. Pulling the door open, there stood my mother, Momma Cha.

"Ma, what are you doing here?"

She smiled and looked at Diamond.

"I hope you didn't think I was going to miss y'all anniversary party!"

She stepped into the bedroom as Diamond tried to cover her body.

"Chile, it ain't like I haven't seen it before," my mother laughed.

"Why didn't you tell me Momma Cha was your mother?" Diamond asked and my mother nudged me in the arm.

"Why have you been keeping me a secret?"

Diamond laughed and I mugged her before laughing myself.

"Ma, get out so my lady can get dressed," I said and pushed her out of the room.

After closing the door, I tried getting Diamond to let me get a nut before leaving, but she wasn't having it.

"No, Kyson. We have to get out of this room," she giggled and walked out.

I heard applause and stepped out right behind her.

"Congratulations bro! You got you a keeper and she bad as fuck, too," my nigga Hassan said as we shook hands. He looked at Diamond's backside and licked his lips, which caused me to laugh.

"Watch how you looking at my girl," I said with a smile but was serious as fuck.

I didn't care who he was. He'd be six feet under if he kept looking at her like that.

"Kyson, you're supposed to be with her," I heard my mother say. I nodded my head before making my way downstairs so I could find my girl.

"Oh Dallas, you need to stop," I heard Diamond laugh. As I walked around the corner, she was standing all in Dallas' face. He had some chick with him but I got pissed off.

I wanted to know who invited the fuck boy to my shit. Pulling Diamond to the side, I was about to dig off in her ass until she spoke.

"I didn't know he was going to be here."

"Well, don't talk to him when you with me."

She looked at me in disbelief but I didn't care.

"You're ridiculous," she said and tried to walk away but I grabbed her hand and stopped her.

"Don't do it. If you know what's best for you, you wouldn't walk away from me," I said with pleading eyes. She sucked her teeth and pulled away from me anyway.

I stood in the middle of the foyer in shock. All I knew was that if I saw her in that fuck nigga's face, I was going beat her ass and kill him. She belonged to me and they knew it. In this last year, he hadn't even been able to get in touch with her.

I posted up at the bar and watch as Diamond and Keisha danced with some other girls then that nigga Dallas was all in her face, trying to get her to walk off with him. Getting up, I made my way over to them when I overheard Diamond say, "Get off me."

"Nah, I need to holla at you real quick," Dallas said and I allowed him to drag her off to one of my guest bedrooms. Los walked up next to me.

"You're not going to go check that shit?"

I nodded and motioned for him to follow me. When we stepped into my office, I opened the doors that were on the armoire and hit the power button. Hitting a few more buttons on the remote I got the camera in the guest bedroom to pull up along with audio.

"Diamond, I miss you," Dallas said.

"I don't miss you, Dallas. And, I would really appreciate it if you leave my house," Diamond said and the nigga tried to kiss her.

She fought him off the first few times then he threw her on the bed and got in between her legs.

I jumped up from my chair and ran to the guest bedroom, barging in.

"Nigga, if you don't get the fuck off my girl!" I yelled with my pistol aimed at him.

Diamond jumped up and ran to my side.

"I got you," I said but before I knew it, this nigga pulled out a gun and let off two shots. It was lights out for me.

12

LOS

Hearing gunshots, I ran into the room. My mouth fell open at the sight before me. There on the floor lay Kyson and Diamond. They both had one gunshot wound to their upper bodies.

"Call 911!" I yelled out and Momma Cha appeared in the doorway along with Diamond's mother and Keisha.

"The paramedics are here!" we heard someone say and moved out of the way before they could push us or tell us to move.

"We have to get them to the hospital," one of the paramedics yelled.

I watched as they carried them out on gurneys one at a time. Keisha and Mrs. Carter rode with Diamond and I climbed into the ambulance with Kyson. My mind was racing. All I could think about was getting at that nigga Dallas for doing this shit.

When we got to the hospital they had us wait in the waiting room Keisha was crying along with Diamonds mother. I was trying to console Keisha when my phone rang. It was Meme, Kyson's baby mother.

"Hello," I answered.

"Los, I heard what happened. Please tell me he's okay?"

This didn't sound like the hood rat ass baby mother he was always talking about. She sounded genuinely concerned.

"We waiting on the doctor now."

"Okay, well keep me updated," she said before hanging up. I sat back and held Keisha.

I was about to go crazy. The wait was getting longer and longer. Getting up I decided to go get some air. I couldn't hear myself think and kept getting this feeling that someone was watching me. Looking up, I spotted a white woman with long blond hair and blue eyes looking at me.

"Wassup ma, what's your name?" I asked, looking into her beautiful eyes.

"Angelica, and you?"

I smirked and shook her hand.

"My name is Los."

As soon as those words left my mouth, Keisha was walking into the waiting room with Momma Cha and her eyes fell on me.

She couldn't even hold the gaze. Before I knew it, tears started falling from her eyes. I stood and made my way over to her.

"It's not what you think, baby."

I tried pleading with Keisha but she didn't even respond. She just turned and walked away from me "The doctors are coming out to talk to us."

"Family of Kyson and Diamond?" the doctor spoke and I jumped up.

"That's us," I said, standing next to the doctor who cleared his throat before speaking.

"Kyson is going to be okay but, Diamond wasn't as lucky."

My heartbeat went back to normal and it felt good knowing my nigga was okay.

"Can I go see him?" I asked the doctor who nodded his head.

I made my way to the back and stopped before walking into the room when I heard Keisha's voice. It sounded urgent so I turned around to face her and she had tears in her eyes.

"Please, tell me she's okay?" I asked while looking into Keisha's eyes that told a different truth.

"What happened?" I asked, sitting down outside of Kyson's room so that he wouldn't see us.

"She's in a coma," Keisha cried and I pulled her into my embrace.

"It's going to be okay. Diamond is a fighter and I know she's going to be okay," I spoke with confidence.

"Now, I need to go talk to my boy and let him know what's going on with his girl."

I kissed her on the cheek before walking into Kyson's room. "Wassup, my nigga?"

"Wassup."

I smiled, happy to see my nigga up and moving around.

"They made it seem like you was dying, nigga," I laughed as I sat next to him.

He shook his head and laughed. "Nigga, you know I ain't going out that easy. But, where my girl?" he asked, looking behind me as Keisha walked into the room.

"Diamond got hit by one of the bullets, too," Keisha informed him.

"Okay, is she dead?" he asked pulling back from Keisha and looking at me for the answer.

"Nah, she not dead. But, she is in a coma and we need your help if she's going to make it," I said, standing up and walking over to Keisha who was about to say something but the nurses came in and put us out.

Keisha and I walked out of the hospital and were met by a woman. "How is my baby?" this stranger asked.

"She's in a coma." Keisha answered.

"Oh my goodness." The woman then took off towards the hospital entrance.

"Who was that?" I asked.

"That's Diamond's father."

I almost threw up in my mouth, which caused Keisha to laugh.

"Oh, you think that's funny?" I said grabbing her and tickling her.

My phone started vibrating as we made our way out of the hospital. I looked at the name that popped up and the screen and quickly pressed the ignore button before Keisha could see it.

"Hmm," I heard her say as she buckled her seatbelt.

"What?" I asked, preparing myself for her to start bitching and nagging about me staying out at all times of the night.

"I just think it's time you and Kyson thought about giving up the drug game. Y'all both have more than enough money to retire," she said.

Instead of entertaining her like I usually do, I just turned up the volume on my radio and rapped along with Kevin Gates new song, *Perfect Imperfection.*

They say my life is amazing
Funny been a question kinda wonder how I made it
Forest Gump and I got something in common
The world treat you different when you make it
We ain't booted off a molly, we don't do shrooms
All we do is pass gas loud, excuse who?

Once I pulled up at the house, my phone started vibrating again. This time it was a 911 from my li'l nigga, Nick, "I need to make a run."

"Really? This late?" she asked with an attitude.

"Keisha, when yo friends call do I stop you? No. I'll be back." I said.

She stomped off and went into the house, slamming the door so hard I heard it.

I called her "Set the alarm and grab my gun out of the sock drawer.

"Okay,"

She hung up in my face.

I was doing everything in my power not to cheat on Keisha. But, she wasn't making it easy. Shawty was too needy and clingy as fuck. I got her that way and now I felt like that wasn't what I wanted anymore. It was okay playing house for the last year and a half but I wasn't feeling her on that level anymore. I had to figure out a way to tell her before it got too out of hand. I didn't want a weak girl. I wanted one who was going to stand up to me and hit my ass back if I hit her.

The trap house looked abandoned when I pulled up to it. All of the soldiers were downstairs in the man cave, which was sound proof. I walked in and the crew was seated in a circle.

"I'm pretty sure you know why we're here." I said, pulling my pistol from my waist and standing in the middle of the room. Everybody started moving their chairs up.

"What I want to know is why I got a 911." I said looking around the room.

The nigga Nick who we put in charge stood up and spoke, "I watched the cameras and saw Lil E and Greg pocket drugs and money."

"Nah, it's not even like that," Greg spoke, standing up and facing me.

"Tell me what it's like then."

I put him in the hot seat with my gun aimed at him. He started sweating bullets and I couldn't hide the smirk that came across my face. I knew I had him and it was a matter of time before he let it spill.

"Lil E started telling us y'all niggas was about to get out of the dope game and that we had to find another way to make ends meets. I didn't want to take your shit and I even put it back," Greg sung like a canary and I looked towards Nick for confirmation and he nodded his head.

I turned around and shot Lil E in the middle of his forehead. His lifeless body fell to the floor. Greg let out a sigh of relief before I turned back towards him and emptied my clip into him.

"You see how he thought he got away with it? Let this be a lesson, never rat on somebody and never bite the hand that feeds you," I said, looking around the room and everyone held the same facial expression. They were shocked.

I watched them clean up the mess before making my way back home to Keisha. I got in the shower. I was in and out in ten minutes and before I knew it, I was walking into my bedroom. I laid on the bed as Keisha scooted next to me.

"I love you."

I knew I shouldn't keep saying it back but I did love shawty. I just didn't think she was the one for me anymore.

"I love you too, ma."

13

KEISHA

Los and I were having our own problems. He didn't want to be with me and I was done with that shit. I have been through so much in my life that I was not in the business to make no nigga be with me. If he wanted to leave his ass can get gone.

I was laying down with my eyes wide open. I couldn't sleep if I tried. This was not how I imagined my life to be. My best friend was in the hospital fighting for her life and I wasn't happy with my situation.

"Los, I think we should just go out separate ways." I finally said.

"If that's what you want."

"It is, I'm not happy and neither are you. I'm tired of you putting your hands on me. Looking at the situation Diamond in I don't want to end up like that." I got up from the bed and started to get dressed.

I couldn't do this anymore. It was time for me to figure out what Keisha needed and I'm the future of Los and I crossed paths well then we'll figure it out.

"Where you going?" he asked sitting up in the bed.

"I'm leaving. You don't want me and I'm tired of trying to make Motherfuckers be with me."

"Keisha, it's not that I don't want to be with you." He stood up out of the bed and walked over to me.

"Los, when you get it together holla at me until then I'm done."

I grabbed my bag and walked out of the bedroom. I didn't want anything from Los.

The only thing I ever wanted was an honest relationship with a man who loved me for me nor someone who used my love against me.

I got into my black Altima and headed to my mother's house. My eyes were finally opened I refused to be in a casket before thirty behind a nigga who didn't want me.

I pulled up into the driveway, parked the car and pulled out the contents to roll me a fat blunt. I usually only smoked with Los but, after tonight's events I need to ease my mind.

After smoking I got out of the car and went into the house.

The next morning, I got up and handled my hygiene before heading out of the house to my car. I was going visit Diamond and tell her everything that transpired. Just because she was in a coma didn't mean she couldn't hear me.

I walked into the hospital making my way to her room I overheard a few nurses saying something about the doctor wanted to keep giving a patient medicine to keep him in a medical induced coma. Shaking my head I just kept on walking.

When I got to diamonds room I saw Kyson sitting next to her in a wheel chair "You shouldn't be out of bed Kyson, you supposed to be resting."

He looked at me "I know what they said but I'm a grown ass man." He said.

"You are really hardheaded you know?" I say down in one of the chairs they had on the other side of the room.

"Only when it comes to Diamond. I just had to come see her. What you doing here so early?"

"I needed to talk to her about something."

"Oh, Aight. Ima give you sometime." He replied then rolled out of the room.

I stood up and walked to her bedside, grabbing her hand I let the tears fall "I think Los and I are done sis. He doesn't want to be with me and I'm tired of getting beat and cheated on. It's like he's doing intentionally so that I would leave. I'm taking that step and saying fuck him. I need to know if you're ready to do the same. I know you love Kyson but, truth be told if you don't leave him you'll end up in a casket. They Don't love us. They love the control sis."

The nurse walked in " I'm sorry but, Ms. Carter isn't supposed to have visitors. The doctor want her to get as much rest as possible me so that she can heal."

"Okay, I'm leaving." I said grabbing my purse and walking out of the room.

I left the hospital and went to meet with a therapist that I was referred to. I had a lot I needed to work through and couldn't do it on my own.

Dallas

I had so many thoughts running through my head as I ran to my car. I didn't mean to shoot Diamond but that nigga Kyson had it coming to him. I was tired of him being in my way. Nadia was blowing my phone up because I ditched her ass. Oh, well. I had to get out of there.

"Hello?" I answered.

"Where the fuck are you?" she screamed into the phone and I couldn't help but laugh at her.

She was always so fucking dramatic.

"Calm the fuck down."

"Hell no, come back and pick me up."

"I can't. Get one of them bitches to drop you off at home," I said and heading to the airport.

I needed to get out of Compton. My phone was ringing continuously by the time I arrived at the terminal. I got on my private jet and took off to New York.

My phone vibrated once more and it was my homeboy, Lenno. "Wassup?" I answered.

"Wassup? Nigga you all over the news."

My mouth dropped open and I turned the news on.

"Dallas Young, 24, is wanted for aggravated assault of an ex-girlfriend and her boyfriend."

I cut the TV off and continued my conversation. "Man, what's the condition?"

I didn't care about what they were talking about.

"The boyfriend is good but Diamond is in a coma."

My head dropped. "What the fuck were you thinking?" Lenno asked.

"I wasn't. Look, I'm headed out of town. I want you to keep me updated on Diamond's condition."

"You know I got you, bro," he said before hanging up.

I had a million thoughts running through my head and one of them was that I knew I fucked up. The vibrating of my phone had it dancing. I had several text messages from Nadia.

Baby momma: *I'm done Dallas. You shot Diamond and Kyson for what?*

Baby momma: *You sorry ass nigga! My kids will never see you again!*

Baby momma: *Sucker ass nigga! I'm taking my kids and leaving your dumbass!*

Baby momma: *Good luck in jail BITCH!*

I couldn't stop laughing. She was funny as hell. I wasn't going to jail and she knew she wasn't going to leave this "sucker ass nigga". I didn't even bother texting her back so I just tossed my phone on the chair and went to the back of the plane to sleep.

"Dallas put the gun down!" Diamond said.

"Nah, this pussy nigga keep standing in the way of us being together." I

had a deranged look in my eyes and the Hennessey shots I had taken didn't make it any better.

"Nigga, put that gun down!"

I took aim. I was tired of that nigga talking so I pulled the trigger.

My eyes popped opened and I was drenched in sweat.

"Now I'm losing sleep behind this shit," I mumbled.

I stood up and made my way to the front to get a pre-rolled blunt and my phone. I had missed calls from Nadia, Keisha, and Jeanette.

I called Jeanette back almost immediately "Dallas, what the fuck?" she yelled into the phone. She had to know I didn't mean to shoot Diamond, but that nigga Kyson was popping off at the mouth too much for me. I was trying to body his ass tonight.

14

JEANETTE

I stood over my daughter's bed. She looked like a vegetable. I couldn't stop the tears that were flowing down my face. I never thought Dallas would be the one to hurt my daughter. I needed to holla at him so I grabbed my iPhone 4s and scrolled down the call log until I saw his name and hit the call button.

"Dallas, what the fuck?" I yelled into the phone when he answered.

"Ma, I'm sorry! I didn't mean to hurt Diamond. Those bullets were meant for that punk ass nigga of hers," he said.

The doorknob started to turn. It was after hours so I was the only one allowed back here.

"Dallas, where are you?" I asked.

"I'm on my way out of town. I need you to nurse Diamond back to health. I'm all over the news. This shit crazy."

"You need to come back and explain what happened running will only make it worse." I said hanging up the phone.

I dropped my phone when the door opened completely. The sight before me had me stunned and horrified.

"Freddy?" I asked.

"No, I go by Cat now, and hello Jeanette."

I didn't know how Diamond was going to take this, but I couldn't wait. I chuckled and sat back in the chair.

"What happened to her?" he asked.

"Um, she's stable but in a coma and she's pregnant, Freddy. So she needs her father, not this," I said in a serious tone.

He looked at me shocked before moving to exit the room.

"I'll leave now but I'll be back," he said and walked his tall frame down the corridor.

I decided to go check on Kyson. He and I needed to have a talk.

"Hey Jeanette," he greeted me. I smiled and nodded my head as I sat in the chair next to his bedside.

"I'm sure they've told you Diamond is expecting again. I mean it when I tell you if any more harm comes to my child you're going to pay."

"I haven't out my hands on diamond. We been good."

"Good, especially since she's pregnant. I'll kill you myself if anything happens to her or my grandbaby."

"Wait, nobody told me she was pregnant." He said.

I nodded. "well, she's pregnant Kyson. You can talk to the doctor tomorrow."

"Okay."

Turning around, I made my way out of his room and back to Diamond's room. To my surprise, she was shifting in the bed in her sleep.

"Mmm."

I heard her groan and rushed over to her.

"Baby girl, are you awake?" I asked and her eyes popped open.

She tried sitting up but the cords that were going inside of her mouth and arms held her down.

"Diamond, stay put. How are you feeling? Are you okay? I thought I lost you. Don't ever scare me like that again." I said kissing her forehead. I ran out of the room and towards the nurses station.

"She's awake!" I yelled and the nurses looked at me like I was crazy.

"She's awake. My daughter, in room 111!"

Once I made it back into the room, she sat up and looked at the doctor.

"Hello, Ms. Carter," the doctor said while flashing a light all into her eyes, causing her to jump back.

"It's okay, you're okay."

The doctor continued before walking out of the room.

"Mom what's going on?" she asked in a raspy voice.

I handed her some water and started explaining everything that happened. "You don't remember any of this?"

She nodded her head then said, "I need to see Kyson."

"That's not possible, Ms. Carter. He can come to you tomorrow but you and the baby are under strict watch," the doctor said as he walked back into the room with an ultrasound machine.

"Would you like to hear the baby's heartbeat?" the doctor asked and Diamond shook her head no.

"Aww, why not?"

"We need to check on the baby."

She crossed her arms and eyed the nurse and doctor before speaking. "Kyson isn't here, get him to me and I'll let you check me."

The doctor looked at me with pleading eyes and I put my hands up and smiled.

"Go get Lions!" she said to the nurse and we walked out of the room.

15

DIAMOND

Waking up, my eyes were blurry and my throat was dry as hell. I tried swallowing but something in my throat wouldn't let me. My eyes fluttered and I heard my mother's voice.

"Baby girl are you awake?"

Opening my eyes, I tried to sit up several times and couldn't because I had tubes coming out of what looked like every hole in my damn body. Before a nurse, my mother and a doctor walked back into the room. The doctor removed the tube that was in my mouth, giving me a glass of water, I sipped on it until my throat started to feel better.

I looked around the room confused and asked, "Ma, what's going on?"

She came and stood next to the bed and started explaining what happened and I was in shock. I couldn't believe Dallas would do something like that because he had never put me in harm's way before.

"You don't remember any of this?" my mother asked.

Shaking my head, I replied, "I need to see Kyson."

After informing them that I wouldn't check up on my baby via ultrasound unless my man was by my side, they finally submitted to my request.

Twenty minutes later, the nurse and my mother came through the door, with Kyson rolling in behind them, smiling from ear to ear. I looked at the nurse who kept touching him. She was pissing me off.

"Let that lady check on my seed, ma," he said and I nodded my head, laid back on the bed, and raised my hospital gown up.

I hated these things because they only gave you one and it had your ass all out. Kyson stood, walked up to me, and took my hand into his.

"Ooh that's cold," I said as the doctor squeezed the clear gel on my stomach before placing the transducer probe and moving it around.

At first, she couldn't locate the heartbeat until Kyson kissed my forehead.

"Stubborn like daddy already," I joked, causing everybody in the room to laugh.

"The baby sounds good. Now you need to get some sleep," the doctor said and motioned for the nurse to take Kyson.

"I'll see you tomorrow," he said and kissed my lips before sitting back in the chair. The nurse, whose nametag read Diane, took my man away.

I laid my head back and drifted off to sleep until I felt my phone vibrate. Looking at the screen, Dallas's name popped up and I polity sent that ass to voicemail. I didn't have anything to say to him and he just needed to respect my wishes. The phone vibrated again and it was him, only this time he sent a text.

Dallas: *I love you. Answer the phone.*

Me: *Really Dallas? You love me but you shot me? Why the fuck did you have a gun any fucking way, dumb ass?*

Dallas: *I always carry my heat and you know that ma. I reacted because yo' nigga pulled his shit first.*

Me: *Just leave me the fuck alone okay Dallas? I'm pregnant by Kyson again and would really appreciate if you would just move the fuck on! Better yet, go back to Nadia.*

I rolled my eyes and closed my phone because I was sure his heart wouldn't be able to handle the fact that I was carrying

Kyson's seed again. Before I could set my phone down, he responded.

Dallas: *You sure about that?*

Me: *What the fuck that's supposed to mean?*

Dallas: *I'm just saying. You nor that nigga faithful ma. You don't love him be honest with yourself. Hit me in nine months ☺*

I was fuming inside. Yeah, we had sex a few times. Kyson was still fucking around on me so I decided to get my payback. I knew I shouldn't have but hell, I couldn't help it and it's not like I just went out and fucked a random nigga. I fucked the only other nigga I had loved. I wished I wasn't in the hospital because I would probably be at his house fucking something up. I released a loud scream and threw my phone on the floor, causing it to crack. Oh, well. A new number was needed anyway. I laid my head back and thought about my life.

In less than a month I would be graduating from high school. I was going to be a mother, and I was the girlfriend to Kyson Lions, one of Compton's biggest dope dealers who was only getting bigger. He traveled from city to city, state to state, and hell sometimes he was even out of the country on business. Sitting up, I grabbed my bag and pulled out my Samsung tablet, looking into some shit for school. I also looked into UCLA, since there was no chance of me leaving Kyson. I planned on going to school for Criminal Law.

The next day, Kyson and I were released. After several attempts of trying to keep us in the hospital, the doctor finally gave in and handed us our release papers.

"You're under strict rules to stay in bed," Kyson said as I got dressed.

I put on some black skinny jeans, a flare baby blue and white strapless shirt, and a pair of sandals.

As soon as we walked out of the hospital, Keisha and Los were there to take us home. I climbed into the car with the help of Kyson and Los.

"Hey, girl," I greeted Keisha, who almost jumped into my arms.

I looked into her eyes that were hiding under shades and knew he was beating her ass again.

She was dressed in a beige maxi dress and some Chanel sandals and her stomach was kind of poking. I made a mental note to talk to her. Kyson climbed in and pulled me next to him, kissing my lips.

"We had to get another spot ma."

I only nodded my head. I knew how it worked. If someone broke into your home or shot you there, you moved because they could always come back to finish the job.

"I texted your phone last night," Keisha said, turning around to look at me.

"It broke."

"Stop somewhere and let me get her another phone," Kyson stated, looking at me with confusion.

Los hopped off the expressway and headed towards a Sprint store. I was nervous just thinking about what Dallas said in those text messages. I sat back in my seat as Kyson ran into Sprint. I thought back to the last time I fucked Dallas. It was maybe a month ago while we were in Houston.

"Diamond we need to go," Dallas said as he tried to pull me off of him but I wrapped my legs around his waist.

I kissed his lips and sucked on his tongue.

"Fuck! Get back," he moaned.

He knew he couldn't resist me and for some reason for that last week, I haven't been able to resist him. Dallas pulled his shirt over my head.

"Mmm," I moaned as he licked and sucked on each of my nipples.

He started kissing down my stomach and made his way to my pussy but not before stopping at my clit. He slowly started licking and sucking on it and I couldn't stop the moans that escaped my mouth.

"Dallas, oh my God! Please don't stop," I moaned as I arched my back and tossed my head back.

Finally, tired of playing with my emotion, he stuck his tongue deep inside of my pussy and started moving it around like a snake. My legs buckled and started shaking before I squirted all over his face.

"Turn over," he demanded.

When I turned, he positioned himself behind me, slapped my ass, and roughly entered me.

"Oh!" I moaned.

He reached around and placed his hand on my mouth. He kept hitting me with deep strokes and I started throwing it back.

He grabbed a fist full of my hair and started pounding me from behind. While my ass was in the air, he took one of his fingers and stuck it in my asshole.

"Ahh!" I moaned but the shit felt like heaven on earth.

"I'm cumin', ma!" he groaned while giving me back shots. I felt his knees buckled and he came.

"Diamond, I love you," he said and ruined the mood.

I stood to my feet and made my way across the room. I walked into the restroom and shut the door behind me. Walking up to the full-length mirror, I looked at myself.

"Is this what you really want? Is it really over between you and Kyson?" I asked myself over and over again. I got my answer when my phone started ringing.

Kyson's name popped up on the screen and I answered.

"Hello."

"You with that nigga, Diamond?" he asked.

When I didn't answer, he continued, "Get your shit and come to room 516."

Before I had a chance to respond, he hung up on me.

When I stepped out of the bathroom, Dallas was gone so I packed my shit, took a shower, and left out.

~

"Diamond?" Kyson asked, snapping me out of my thoughts as he handed me my new iPhone 6 plus. I leaned over and kissed him. I had a moment of weakness when I fucked Dallas. I'd be devastated if I learned that he was the father of my child. It's not like Kyson was any better but he's trying.

The rest of the drive to the house was quiet besides a conversation between Kyson and Los about something that happened at one of the trap houses.

"Baby, you good?" Kyson asked as he rubbed my stomach, which was weird.

I never forgave him for making me lose our first son, who I named Kendrick Mason Lions. I nodded my head as a tear fell from my eye and he pulled me into a hug.

"I'm sorry," he apologized as if he knew exactly what I was crying about.

Pulling up to the new house was a relief. It was much bigger and it sat on its own land in the boondocks. The circular driveway, freshly manicured lawn, and the house was breathtaking. Walking up, I admired the cars that sat in the driveway and noticed a brand new custom pink two-door BMW.

"That's for you, ma," Kyson said as he walked me over to the car and pulled the door open for me.

I got in and instantly fell in love. The black leather interior was everything and the seats had a D engraved into them in gold lettering.

I got out of the car and grabbed Kyson's hand. Standing in front of him, I kissed his lips.

"Thank you, baby. I love it!"

"No need to thank me. You deserve it," he responded as we entered the house and Momma Cha, Talia, and my mother. The foyer was beautiful. There was a round table sitting in the middle of the floor with a huge flower arrangement. Our car keys along with some unopened mail were sitting on the table, too.

There was a huge chandelier on the ceiling that had little crystals hanging from it. We walked into the living room and it was all-white.

"Brave."

I took my shoes off and stepped on the plush white carpet.

"What you said?" Keisha asked.

I looked at her and smiled as she hugged me again.

"I said this is brave. As in the color."

I looked back at Kyson, who was sitting in the kitchen with Los.

The living room had a White sectional that sat at least eight people, white overthrow pillows, and a coffee table.

Walking out of the living room, Keisha and I made our way upstairs, which was the perfect time to talk to her. We stepped into the master bedroom and I closed the door behind us. I was amazed at the bedroom. The king-sized bed, the balcony, and sixty-inch television took me by surprise.

"Are you pregnant?" I asked.

"Yes."

"Does Los know?" I asked and her face dropped.

She removed her sunglasses and said, "Last night we got into a huge fight because I went through his phone and he's still fucking with that ratchet ass ex of his."

Shaking my head, I replied, "You need to tell him, Kee. You can do it while y'all are here."

She shook her head.

"Come with me," she said and we walked out of the room and made our way back downstairs.

"Where's Los?" Keisha asked Kyson.

She looked back at me and we made our way to the kitchen where Los was eating a sandwich.

"Hey baby, I need to talk to you."

"Okay," he replied but never looked at her, which was pissing me off.

"Look, Los, you need to put the fucking sandwich down and pay the fuck attention," I said, slapping the sandwich out of his hand.

"Yo, for real D? Kyson, come get your girl!"

Kyson came running into the kitchen. "Diamond, stay out of it."

"Tell him, Keisha," I said and everybody turned her way.

"I'm pregnant," Keisha said and Los slumped into his chair.

I turned and walked out of the kitchen when someone knocked on the door.

16

KYSON

I was finally getting another chance at being a father and I couldn't be any happier. When the nurse and Jeanette came into my room, I was surprised as hell to see them again.

"Jeanette, what's going on?" I asked as the nurse grabbed my IV pole and told me to get up and go with them.

"Diamond won't let the doctor check on the baby unless you're there."

A part of me was pissed off at her for that and another was happy that she wanted to wait for me to hear the baby's heartbeat. As they rolled me down the hallway, I couldn't help but think of all the things I wanted to be different with Diamond this pregnancy. I wanted to be there every step of the way.

After being brought back to my room, I was exhausted and was in a little pain so the nurse gave me some morphine but what I needed was marijuana. I laughed to myself and laid down.

"You okay?" the nurse asked and I had to admit she was bad.

"Nah, you can go," I said and she pulled the covers over me but not before grabbing my erect dick.

"I'm sorry," she smirked.

I wasn't really feeling her touching me.

"Yeah, just go," I said in a cold tone and she left the room with an attitude, but I didn't give a fuck.

I belonged to Diamond Carter, who was soon to be Mrs. Lions and she didn't even know it.

I rolled over and felt my eyes get heavy. Before I knew it, I was out.

The next morning, I woke up to the sound of my mother's and Talia's voice.

"Kyson, wake up," she said, causing me to immediately jump back.

"Talia, what the fuck?"

"Sorry cuz," she apologized as she helped me up.

"Did they give us our release papers yet?" I asked, noticing it was going on twelve in the afternoon.

"Not yet. But, I'm on my way up to go see the doctor now," Momma Cha said as she walked out of the room with Talia behind her.

I lay back on the bed and waited for them to come back, which was a half an hour later.

I threw on some gray sweatpants, a black T-shirt, and a pair of Nike slides. I looked in the mirror and ran my hands over my waves. Walking out of the restroom, Diamond, Keisha, and Los were already in my room.

"Where did my mom go?" I asked.

"She and Talia headed to the house. I told her I'd take y'all home," Los said as he grabbed Diamond's wheelchair and proceeded to push her.

"I got it," I said and Los moved.

When we made it home, a nigga was tired than a motherfucker. I needed to regain my strength because I had business in the streets to take care of. I most definitely couldn't wait for that pussy Dallas to show his face around because I was going to light his ass up.

When my phone started vibrating, I looked at the Caller ID and saw that it was Meme calling.

"Yo!" I answered.

"Kyson? Oh good, you must be home. Can I come over and talk to you?" she asked.

At first, I was hesitant but eventually gave in.

"Alright," I said before ending the call.

I texted her the address and then went upstairs to check on Diamond.

"What?" Diamond asked as I stood in the doorway of our bedroom and stared at her.

She was beautiful and I would be a fool to give her up. I walked up to her and got down on one knee in front of her. "Kyson, what are you doing?" She asked moving back on the bed.

"Diamond Nyla, I love you with everything in me. I can't see myself without you. I'll jump in front of a bullet for you, ma. You're carrying my seed again, too. I feel like I'm where I'm supposed to be. Will you marry me?" I asked opening the small black box that carried her round cut 9 karat engagement ring.

She nodded as tears cascaded down her cheeks.

"Say it ma."

"Yes, Kyson! I'll marry you!" she yelled excitedly and jumped in my lap. I said the ring on her finger.

We kissed with so much passion. I stood up and laid her on the bed and tried to remove her blue jeans.

My phone started vibrating and it was Meme telling me to come downstairs.

"My baby momma is here. She wants to talk to me," I said and walked out of the room.

Not even ten minutes later, Diamond and Keisha came walking into the living room looking like they were on a mission. I just hoped whatever it was, Diamond would mind her fucking business.

"Where is Los?" Keisha asked and I pointed towards the kitchen.

I took notice of Keisha's weight gain over the past three months but said nothing about it. I looked at Diamond then Keisha before they marched into the kitchen.

17

MEME

The day I got the phone call from Erica telling me Kyson got shot, I made up my mind that I wanted my baby's dad back. He could talk all the shit he wanted to, but he knew where the fuck his heart was and that was with me and our daughter, Kalani. Kyson and I were high school sweethearts so I didn't get why he consistently lied, telling people I was just a drunk one-night stand that went wrong.

After Kyson gave me his address, I grabbed a peach colored high waist pencil skirt, button up white blouse, and Red Bottom peep-toe heels. I grabbed my Michael Kors bag, keys, and walked out of the front door. I hopped into my white BMW and drove off.

I plugged my iPhone 5s up to my auxiliary cord and scrolled down my music to Future's *Throw Away* and sung along with him.

Does Sexing on a late night mean that much to ya?
My love don't mean that much ya
Fucking these hoes meant too damn much to ya
I just hope when you fuck another nigga
When you finished
He can say that he love ya

Now do you feel better about yourself?

Forty-five minutes later, I was standing in his living room about to pour my whole heart out to him when Diamond walked around the corner.

"Meme, you remember my fiancé? Diamond?." He asked me.

"Fiancé?"

My hands were trembling and I felt myself becoming consumed with anger.

"Kyson, can we talk alone?"

"I wasn't staying in here anyway. I got better things to do." Diamond said walking into the kitchen with another chick.

I rolled my eyes at her then turned my attention back to Kyson.

"When did this happen?" I asked.

"Look, Meme, we had fun when Diamond was fucking with that fuck boy, Dallas. But, this is my home and that's my girl. She's taking care of our daughter plus she's carrying my seed."

My heart shattered into pieces. Kyson promised me that I would be the only woman carrying his children but he lied because this little bitch was now pregnant and engaged to the man I loved. I felt my blood boiling as she walked back into the living room holding Lani before sitting her in her high chair to eat. I ran towards her at full speed and pushed her to the floor.

"Bitch!" I yelled and was about to kick her in the stomach until Kyson rushed me and knocked me into the wall.

"Get the fuck out of my house!" he yelled with venom.

I knew I had just fucked up but I wasn't thinking.

"Kyson, I'm in love with you," I confessed.

"Get the fuck out!" he said through clenched teeth.

I looked at him with tears in my eyes but remained silent. I made my way towards the front door and walked out.

Getting into my car, I couldn't help the tears that escaped from my eyes. Kyson was my first everything. He was the first boy I ever dated, the first boy I kissed, and the first boy I had sex with. Now my first and only love was engaged and having a baby with another woman.

Well, that shit was not happening on my watch. She could have the baby, but the wedding wasn't happening. Hell, just before their little anniversary party, Kyson was swimming in my pussy. He could play like he didn't love me but we both knew he did.

I decided to go to the club because I needed a drink. Pulling up to Club Flashy, I stopped at the valet and tossed my keys to the attendant before making way right into the club VIP section.

I was now dressed in a black mini skirt, a red bra with rhinestones, and topped the outfit off with a pair of Givenchy peep-toe heels.

"Meme!" I heard someone yelled as I walked through VIP.

Turning, I saw that it was Erica and Shaela.

"Hey, y'all."

They had another chick with them but for some reason, she kept mugging me.

"Hi, I'm...," before I could say my name, the chick punched me dead in the face

WHAM! WHAM!

Her punches were coming so fast that I could barely compose myself. I finally felt somebody pulling her off of me but I couldn't move.

"We need to get her to the hospital!" I heard Erica yell as she helped me up off the ground.

"I'm good E. I can drive myself," I said as I stumbled out of the club.

Erica helped me into the passenger seat and jumped in the drivers seat. My head was bleeding profusely and it felt like my nose was broken.

Pulling up to the Emergency Room, she parked in front of the emergency doors and helped me out "I'm going to go park."

I walked into the hospital and it was packed. I got dizzy and tried to grab a hold of a chair but, was too late. I fell on my ass.

"Ma'am are you alright?" a young nurse with pale, white skin and curly hair asked rushing over to help me up.

I shook my head no and felt my body giving up.

"We need help!" I heard the nurse yell before my eyes closed.

18

KEISHA

I was hyped that was my first fight in along time. That bitch had it coming it wasn't cool to jump on a pregnant girl especially my friend. I will die defending my bitch. Why? Cause that my bitch.

I sipped on my bottle of water and watched as they took Meme to the exit. I smiled at my work. She deserves every bit of that ass beating.

"Why the fuck are you out here fighting and shit like you're not pregnant with my seed?" he asked as I tried to walk away from him.

"Yo, ma, you need a ride home?" a random man asked.

"Get in the fucking car, Keisha!" Los snapped and I decided not to take my chances and just got into the car.

"Los, we not even together anymore so why the fuck are you in my space. I don't need a ride home from you or any other nigga." I snapped.

I walked off and got into my car. Starting the car I jammed to my music and made my way home.

I hated the fact I was pregnant and by Los at that. We haven't been with each other since the night I left him. I was doing good without him.

I didn't need him and neither did my child.

19

MAYA

I was going to make Los pay if he thought he was just going to leave me alone. I loved him, of it wasn't for Keisha we would probably still be together.

I was going to pay that little bitch a visit, too. When she got a whiff of me, she was going to really be out of his life. Fuck her and that baby.

"Los, this is the fifth voicemail I've left. I need to talk to you."

I wasn't about to just let her come in and ruin what we had. Nope, that was not going to happen.

My phone vibrated, interrupting my thoughts. It was my cousin, Seven.

"Hello," I answered.

"Cuz, wassup? I found that chick Keisha."

I sat up in my bed because he had my full and undivided attention.

"Okay?"

"She and Los are having major issues. I think he's been beating that ass."

I looked at the phone thinking he couldn't be talking about the same Los that I dated back in high school up until he got with Keisha.

"Nah, Los would never."

"How well do you know this nigga?" Seven asked.

I rolled my eyes. Although he was my older cousin, he was not my daddy.

"Seven, mind your business."

"Shit, I'm just asking."

Seven was the weed plug in Cali. Anything you wanted, he had. The nigga had hoes for days, too. He literally had a different girl that would be living in his house every morning. I was surprised that he didn't have a baby on the way with the hood rats he fucked with.

"Okay, don't," I said before I hung up the phone.

I called Keisha's phone.

It rang twice before Los picked up.

"Maya, if you don't stop calling my fucking girl's phone, I'm going to hurt you."

Before I had a chance to respond, he hung up. I started laughing hysterically at Los. At one point, he thought I was the one and now he was acting like I never mattered to him.

"Oh, I'm going to show him."

I stood up and walked into my closet. I dressed in a pair of black skinny jeans, a white crop top, and some black Givenchy boots. I grabbed my Gucci bag and keys and walked out the door.

Jumping into my black Audi, I made my way to his house. When I turned on their street, I noticed Kyson's Tahoe sitting in the driveway I stopped at the end of the street and waited for his add to leave. Kyson is Ochocino with the hands. He didn't give fuck. He would beat a bitch ass with no problems so it was no way I was going over there and show my ass in his presence.

I leaned down in my chair when I saw them emerge from the house.

"Bitch, it's time." I said to myself.

I watched them talk for a while before Kyson drove off. Doing seventy I tried to run Los bitch ass over but, he jumped out of the way.

"What the fuck?!" I heard his ask out loud.

I got out of my car with a bat in my hand "Since you forgot who I am let me remind you nigga."

I swung the bat connecting with his stomach and he instantly dropped to the ground. Dropping it, I locked him in his head and sat on top of him.

"Why would you choose that weak ass bitch over me? I loved you! I really fucking loved you!" I screamed at the top of my lungs while punching him.

I was trying to make him feel the same pain I felt when I found out about him and Keisha fucking around while we were in a relationship.

"Are you taking your medication?" he asked flipping me over. He pinned my arms to the ground before getting up.

"Fuck that medicine."

"You know your ass2 is passed crazy right?" he asked out of breath.

"You got me this way. What you mean?"

I got up from the ground and tried to hit him again but, he blocked it and punched me the nose.

"Oweeeee." I winced in pain.

"Maya, stay the fuck away from me. Okay?" Do you hear me? I will kill you bitch."

He walked away leaving me standing in his driveway.

20

LOS

Maya had me all the way fucked up, I was a crazy ass nigga and we both know of I wanted to kill her add last night it wasn't nothing.

"Yo what happened? I see tire marks all on the grass and shit." Kyson said just walking in my house. I could of been trying to get some pussy from a bitch.

"That bitch Maya. That's what happened. That how still in her feelings because I broke up with her and now I see why. She tried to run my ass over and she hit me with a damn bat bruh."

"Oh shit!" Kyson laughed.

This shit was so funny to him but, it wasn't.

"This shit not funny. I got whiplash fucking with her."

"That bitch just as crazy as yo ass." He laughed harder.

I knew her heart was broke after what I did but, damn she really tried to kill my ass. Being off her meds played a major part, she was diagnosed with a bipolar disorder back in high school after getting expelled for pushing a bitch down the stairs.

"Man she love yo ass. You made that bitch crazy."

"She said the same thing." I chuckled.

I grabbed a blunt and fired it up. We was still looking for this bitch ass nigga Dallas. It was like his pussy ass just disappeared.

"Any word on Dallas whereabouts?"

"Not yet."

I passed him the blunt before getting up to grab all the paper work my Private investigator had dug up on his ass.

"He got kids?" Kyson asked looking at the pictures.

"Same thing I said." I said standing up. I needed to give Keisha a call just to make sure this crazy bitch didn't try to fuck with her and my seed.

"Hmm. I could go after the baby momma and kids. That'll get his attention."

"Nah man, them kids innocent."

I wasn't in the business of fucking with people kid a and he shouldn't be either considering he have a daughter and Diamond is pregnant with his seed.

"I be right back."

I got up and went into the kitchen with the phone to my ear. It rang twice before Keisha answered "Hello."

"You good?" I asked sitting on the counter with a beer in my hands.

"I'm straight. That bitch Maya keep playing on my phone. I'ma beat her add if I see her." She said into the phone.

"No you not. Stay yo ass I'm the house while you pregnant with my seed. I don't need nothing happening to you or the baby. I'll handle Maya."

"Oh, like you been handling her?" she said with an attitude.

"Man bye." I hung up the phone on her and went back into the living room.

Kyson was on the phone with somebody and told me not to say anything. I wanted to blow up his shit giving me order like this ain't my house.

He finally got off the phone "My niggas got eyes on Dallas in New York. I told them not to do anything until I came. You rolling?"

"I need to handle Maya before she try to harm Keisha and my

baby. You might want to do they same you know she and Meme roll together."

"Nah, I been out a end to that friendship. Maya used to have Meme doing some ducked up shit." he chuckled.

"True that shit. I used to want to strangle them bitches." I laughed.

"No lie. I need to get out of here. Diamond in one her moods and I need to go cheer her up so I can sneak away and go to New York."

"Yea, cause she ain't letting you go no where."

I walked with him outside and noticed my range rover had been keyed with the word bitch on the hood.

"This bitch not playing. You better kill her ass and soon."

"Oh, don't worry. I'm about to head over to see her ass right now." I said pissed off.

I ran into the house and grabbed my car keys. I got into the car and drove the hour ride to her house. This shit was about to come to an end, she was either about to die and leave the state all together. I wanted no need her Looney add away from me, Keisha and our seed.

21

DALLAS

Every since the shooting I been laying low in New York at my father's estate. I never left the house. If I needed to have business meetings they were to come here. I knew it wouldn't long before Kyson or his boys found me and killed me. I wasn't scared I stayed with a pistol on me just in case.

I was sitting in the kitchen with my mother, Brenda while she cooked. I was happy to be back home. I was only in Compton for Diamond and got into all this shit. This wasn't how it was supposed to go.

"Dallas, come to my office boy." Kapo, my father said walking passed the kitchen.

"For what?"

I never talked to him unless it was concerning business. That's the only relationship I had with this nigga.

"If you don't want bullet in yo add I suggest you get you dumb ass in here boy."

My momma looked and me and said "Go head."

I got up from the chair and put my blunt I was smoking in my mouth. To have a conversation with him, I d to smoke about three blunts.

"This beef between you and Kyson, end it," he said as soon as I stepped into his office and shut the door behind me.

"Not until I get my girl back."

"Nigga, fuck that black bitch."

"Fuck you! Don't disrespect her pops."

I swear sometimes I hated that nigga with everything in me. I wanted to kill this nigga. Why you so worried about that fuck nigga and me?

He sighed before taking a seat in the big leather chair that sat behind his desk. "Kyson is, in fact, your brother and I need you two on the same page before shit gets too sour.

I was in a daze and utterly confused. What the fuck did he mean Kyson was my brother?

I stood and walked to the door. "Pops, you're bugging. Ain't shit over. That nigga will never be my brother."

"You still more worried about pussy then getting money. I see."

I squinted my eyes at my father, trying to understand if I heard him correctly.

"My money long. It's only one pussy I'm worried about, she ain't none of your concern. This between me and Kyson."

"That's where you're wrong son. Kyson is also making money with me so it is my business. He brings me almost as much money as you do." Kapo stood up and walked around his desk. "There should be a simple solution instead of you two trying to kill each other behind some pussy."

WHAM!

I punched him in the jar and sent him flying across the room.

I was tired of him disrespecting what Diamond meant to me. She was more than just a piece of pussy. She had my heart. I needed her more than life it's self.

Walking out of the office I slammed his door behind me and left the house. If Kyson was going to kill me he better take his chance now because I was coming for him. Brother or not.

22

MEME

After getting my ass whipped by Keisha, I decided to leave Kyson alone for the time being. But, he couldn't ignore me forever and we both knew that.

A few days ago, Maya, but me up talking about going have drinks. It was odd and put out of the blue considering Kyson made me stop talking to her back in high school.

I was standing in the mirror putting the finishing touches on my makeup when a horn honked.

I walked outside and locked my house up. When I got into her black Audi, she tried to lean in for a hug but I stopped that ass right in her tracks.

"What's up with the out the blue call? We don't fuck with each other like that."

"Damn, can you pretend to be happy to see a bitch?"

"No, ma'am. But, wassup?"

"I wanted to talk to you about Kyson and Diamond."

"Nah, I'm good on him and her. I just needed a good time," I smiled and sat back as she took off towards a reggae club called Twans.

"This place stay packed," I said as I stepped out of her car.

I frowned my face up in disappointment because the line that was wrapped around the brown brick building. I looked at her and she smirked.

"Girl, we ain't waiting in no damn line. My cousin owns this place."

Maya pulled out her cell phone and called her cousin and we were let in immediately.

"Wassup?" her cousin asked.

He was fine as hell.

"Hi," I said, dryly.

He was dressed in black Prada slacks, a short sleeve button up shirt, and black Prada shoes. His haircut was short and his tattoos were visible.

"You shy?" he asked with raised eyebrows.

"Not at all. Just get a few drinks in her," Maya yelled out.

I wanted to punch this bitch in her throat. "Excuse me, bitch. You don't know me at all. I'm not like that at all."

"What's your name?"

"Mekayla. But, I go by Meme. What's yours?" I batted my long eyelashes at him.

"Seven," he said, causing me to chuckle.

"That's your real name?"

"Yeah, my mother couldn't think of anything else to name me so she named me Seven."

He wasn't smiling so I knew he was telling the truth. He led us to the VIP lounge and had a section waiting for us with bottles.

"Can I get you anything else?" the fine ass Bartender asked.

She had long blond hair and perky titties that were hanging out the front of her crop top that read Twans across it.

"No, thank you Chelsea." Seven answered for me.

I watched as Tatiyana walked into the VIP section with her sisters, Skylor and Kaia.

"Meme? Maya?" she smirked and sat in one of the chairs on the other side of the room.

I couldn't understand her beef with me and really didn't give a damn about it. She wasn't paying any of my bills so she can keep that beef right over there.

"You know her?" Maya asked.

I nodded and grabbed the glass of champagne from Seven. I couldn't understand why he was all in my face of he had a club to run. I was so good on any other nigga who wasn't Kyson.

"We need something stronger than this cousin. Where the Hennessey?" Maya asked sitting the champagne glass down.

I nodded my head "Yeah, this shit not doing nothing for me." I laughed.

Tatiyana was staring at me and testing on her phone.

"Yo, is it me or is this bitch asking for an issue?" Maya asked.

I shrugged my shoulders. Tatiyana was far from just a pretty face, that bitch will do some damage. I fought her in high school thinking she and Kyson had something going on and she beat my ass black and blue. I missed school for a while month because of that ass whopping.

Finally Seven walked back into the lounge with a bottle of Hennessey and Vodka. He opened the bottles and poured me a shot of both drinks mixed.

Taking the shot, I instantly got hot. This was about to be one ducked up night for me but, I planned to play it safe. Maya had no sympathy and I could tell she was off her meds. I wasn't trying to get in no bullshit with this unstable ass bitch.

23

DIAMOND

"Why is Meme still calling your phone Kyson?" I asked. We were laying in the bed and I just couldn't keep my mouth shut any longer. Closed mouths don't get fed.

"I don't know. I haven't read the messages." He was lying straight to my face.

"Nigga, you a motherfucking lie. It ain't no way in hell."

"If you don't stop yelling. You gone get fucked up."

"You thought. Put ya hands on me I swear to God I'll kill yo black ass." I said sitting up.

"Look, she been begging me to come to her house and shit. I went to go check on her. That's it I promise."

"Do you love her Kyson? I need to know why you so dumb stupid? This bitch tried to jump on me and you going check on her? For real?" I asked.

"Of course I do, she's the mother of my child," he answered.

I cocked my head to the side and laughed. "Fuck out of here with that bullshit. You know what I mean."

"Watch yo' tone, ma."

I smirked and backed up until I was on the other side of the room. "Yeah, I know how you get. But, answer me."

When I said that, he looked hurt and I felt like shit. He grabbed his keys and was about to walk out the door, but he turned around and started walking back towards me. He picked me up and threw me on the bed.

"Is this what you want?" he asked, pulling my shirt over my head and unsnapping my bra.

"Mmm," I moaned as he pulled one of my nipples into his mouth and sucked on it while softly pinching the other one.

I threw my head back and arched my back.

"Diamond, I love you and only you. Okay?" He asked while switching breasts and unbuttoning my shorts at the same time.

I ignored him.

"Answer me."

"Ky-Kyson!" I moaned a little too loud.

"Yeah, I like that shit," he moaned, roughly pulling my panties off.

This shit had me wet and horny as fuck.

"Touch it, ma."

I turned to face him and took him into my mouth.

"Yeah just like that," he moaned as he started pumping in and out of my mouth.

He bent me over and stuck one of his fingers into my pussy and started roughly moving it in and out of me.

"Oh my God," I moaned out loud as he started playing with my clit.

"Ooh, I'm cumming," he groaned and shot his seed down my throat.

"Come here," he demanded and I crawled to the edge of my bed.

He pushed me back and stuck his head in between my legs and started eating my pussy.

"Kyson!" I screamed as he sucked, slurped, and licked on my pussy.

"You like that?" he asked as he inserted two fingers into my honey pot.

I nodded before squirting all over his face.

"Oh, my God!" I moaned and before I could catch my breath, Kyson was sliding all ten inches of him inside of me.

"Ahh!" I moaned out as he started hitting me with long strokes. "Daddy is going to take care of that pussy."

"Mhm," was the only thing I could muster up to say.

He was hitting all of my spots with every stroke he delivered to the point where I felt my knees go weak. This was truly the man I wanted to spend the rest of my life with and I was going to do that sooner than I thought.

The fact that Dallas called last night saying we needed to talk, had me thinking about the future Kyson and I were going to have soon. I was going to stay away from him.

The next morning, I woke up to breakfast in bed and Lani kissing all over my face.

"Good morning, ma," Kyson said, exiting the bathroom with just a towel wrapped around his waist. I caught a glimpse of my name tattooed down his spine.

"Kyson, is that my name tatted?"

Nodding, he walked into the closet and came out dressed in some black Levi's, a red Chicago Bulls shirt, and red and black Jordan's.

"Where are you going?" I asked.

"We're supposed to be getting ready to go out of town."

I got excited. Kyson and I hadn't been out of state together in a while.

"Well, I need to go somewhere first," I said, jumping of bed and going into the restroom to get myself together.

I dressed in white ripped skinny jeans, that I could barely get my ass into, a loose beige v neck shirt and some black Chanel sandals. I pulled my hair back into a ponytail that was hanging over my shoulder.

"Where is that?"

"To see Keisha. I haven't talked to her in a few days. I'm worried about her."

I grabbed my car keys but, Kyson stopped me.

"You not driving no where."

"Well, you going to drive me?"

"Do I look like a cab?" His smart ass asked.

"As a matter of fact you do. Come on now."

I grabbed my cell phone and started to walk down stairs. The last thing Keisha told me was that, that bitch Maya was playing on her phone and saying she was going to do something to her child.

Kyson and I got into his red Benz and headed for her house. Everything was going so good between us before Meme came back in hollering about she loved him. I didn't understand why she just couldn't let him be where he was. I was almost to do the point of letting her ass have him. If she wanted the money and ass whippings I out up with before actually being happy. She can have all that shit.

I heard everything Keisha was saying when I was in a coma. We both had a whole life ahead of us but, I was in too deep with Kyson. I was truly in love. He had my heart, mind and soul. It wasn't going to nearly as easy to leave Kyson as it was for her to leave Los.

We pulled into her driveway and her car was parked along with a white range rover. I got out with Kyson.

Knocking on her front door there was a long pause before it opened and Los was standing there with a bandage around his arm.

"What the fuck happened?"

"That bitch happened. She shot me."

"Oh my God! Is Keisha okay?" I asked pushing passed him and into the house. "Keisha!" I yelled.

" I'm in the kitchen. Why yo ass yelling?"

"Bitch, because I thought something happened to you. I see Los with a bandage around his arm."

I sat down on stool across from her.

"That crazy ass ex of his had somebody shoot up his house." She seemed to calm for me.

I laughed "These niggas met they matches I see. Meme and Maya some fucked up ass bitches."

"Girl! I'm learning a thing or two on how to handle Los, because of he think I'm going to take another ass whopping he got another thing coming. I promise you that."

"Y'all back together?' I asked with my head cocked to the side.

"No ma'am."

"Might as well be."

"Hell no. Enough about us, have you and Kyson started planning the wedding?"

I put my head down "No, it ain't gone be a wedding if Meme is still going to be in the picture. He run every time the bitch calls and claim it's because she his daughters mother. She be blowing this nigga up like they still fucking."

"I don't get niggas like him. He have a whole woman out here he engaged to and he still worried about his trifling ass baby mama, who don't even have the baby?" she shook her head.

"I'm so tired of this shit and he think sex is just the answer to all of our problems. It's not." I truthfully stated.

"Friend, its okay to let that nigga know you not taking this shit no more. It's time for Diamond to figure out what makes Diamond happy. If you think you need that nigga to take care of that child think again cause you don't. If he don't respect y'all relationship you can't expect a bitch to sis." Keisha was right. Kyson was either going to be all for me or not for me at all. I'm not into sharing my husband.

I was about to put my big girl panties on and let this nigga know what the fuck it was. We wasn't going on no trip until he figured this shut out. I'm tired of being lied to.

24

CHANEL (MOMMA CHA)

I spent most of the time minding my business but, now that Kyson and Diamond were engaged it was time for me to have a conversation with her. I knew they had issues as far as him putting his hands on her and numerous of times I told him that girl is going to get tired of that shit. I went through this same shit with his father.

I was one in the same getting my ass beat. He belittled me. Abuse is not just about physical abuse it's emotional and verbal abuse also. I loved Diamond like she was my daughter so it was time for me to step in because of she didn't want to marry him we can do what was necessary to get her and that baby away from him.

I tried getting Kyson help a long time ago but, Kapo shut it down saying his son didn't need help. The bitches he fucked with was always doing something to provoke him.

I was on my to Diamond and Kyson's house when my phone started to ring. It was Kapo.

"Who is this?" I answered playing it off like I didn't know who it was.

"Chanel, stop playing."

"What the hell you calling me for?" I asked turning on Kyson street.

"You. Come visit me."

I pulled the phone away from my face and looked at it.

"Nigga, bye." I said hanging up. He had me fucked up. This nigga was married and some more shit. I be damned I feel for that again.

After parking my car, I got out and walked up to the front door. I knocked twice and waited for somebody to answer "Who is it?"

"Momma cha." I said and the door opened. Diamond was starting to get bigger and bigger and I couldn't wait for her to find out if she was giving me a grandson or daughter.

"What you doing here?" She asked.

"We need to talk."

She moved to the side and let me into the house. We went into the living room and say down and I got straight to the point "Do my son make you happy?"

"Yes ma'am."

"Are you happy? Tell me the truth."

She took a deep breath "As of now I don't know. I'm not planning a wedding because this situation with him and Meme is very dangerous. She texted his phone saying she was going to do whatever it takes to get this wedding stopped. He run every time she calls. She shouldn't be calling him when she doing even have the child. I'm taking care of her."

I nodded my head.

"Well baby, if you aren't happy you need to leave Kyson ass alone. I don't know what made you stay after he out his hands on you because I would of chopped his damn hands all the way off."

She laughed.

"Its not funny. You are too pretty to be putting up with this shit. I don't care that he is my son some shit needs to be stopped."

I shifted in the sofa and looked into her eyes. I really wanted her to get it through that head of hers that she didn't have to put up with this shit.

"Do you want to die?"

"Huh?"

She had a confused look on her face.

"Do you want to die? Because that's what's going to happen if you don't see the light and leave Kyson alone. My son is unstable and been this way for a long time. I tried getting him help but, his father beat my ass because he couldn't stand the fact that I knew my child better than he did."

"Whoa, I had no idea."

"Now you do. I love my son with everything in me but, he not right. I just don't understand why you staying with him."

"Because I love him." Diamond said throwing me for a loop.

"Love is not broken ribs. Busted lips or a bruised ego. I want you to think about that before marrying him. Okay?"

She nodded her head.

"Yes, I get what you saying."

"I hope you do. I would hate to at your funeral and you're not even thirty yet."

I hugged her and headed for the front door.

"Yes ma'am. You be careful." She said walking me to my car.

"You be careful."

I got into my car and drive out of the driveway. I was hoping she kept this conversation between us two ladies. I also hopes she was actually listening to to my words.

25

SHAELA

"I can not believe Diamond is engaged to Kyson." Erica said.

I rolled my eyes I was getting so tired of her. All she wanted to do was talk about Diamond and Kyson. She had a personal beef with diamond. It was like she wanted everything she had just to say she did it.

"As much as he used to beat her ass." She snickered. That was the last straw for me.

"Let's not forget we were in their shoes at one point, too."

I thought back on the time Kai beat my ass for showing up at his baby mother's house.

~

I was eighteen-years old and we'd just made one year in our relationship, but Kai wasn't home and hadn't been home in several days.

"This is Kai, leave a message," I hung up and threw my phone across the room.

"Ugh!" I sat down and my mind started racing.

I stood, grabbed my keys and purse, and walked out of the two-story brownstone that we owned.

I got into my 2014 white BMW and made my way to Kai's baby mother, Kyndell's, home. He was forever over there claiming he was seeing his son, but the pictures on Facebook told a different story. When I pulled up and climbed out of my car, I saw his Ford truck and pulled out my pocket knife.

"Since you wanna layup with this bitch..." I said before I slashed all four of his tires.

I walked back to my car, popped the trunk, and pulled out my metal baseball bat.

BAM! BAM!

As I smashed the windows out, the front door flew opened and Kai snatched my ass right up.

"Get the fuck on!"

I stumbled back until I lost my balance and fell on my ass.

"Shaela, I'm about to beat yo' ass!"

Standing, I tried to run to the car but he grabbed me and slammed me into the window of my car before he threw his arm back and started backhanding me.

WHAP! WHAP! WHAP! WHAP!

I couldn't stop him so I started screaming.

"Kai, stop! Stop!" he spat as his fist collided with my cheek.

WHAM!

I fell to the ground, bleeding profusely. Lying in the fetal position in the middle of the street, he proceeded to step over me, but not before he delivered two hard kicks to my abdomen.

"Argh!"

The pain was unbearable.

"P-p-pl-please," I stammered.

"Please, what?" Kai asked as he grabbed a fist full of my hair and drug me to the passenger's side of the car.

"Get in!"

The drive to the house was the worst ride of my life. Kai kept on beating me.

WHAP!

I grabbed my face and looked at him with tears in my eyes. I was starting to hate him and he knew that. It was almost as if that was what he wanted. When we pulled into the driveway, I held my face so that his friend wouldn't see it. She had been telling me I needed to get away from Kai's crazy ass.

I ran up the stairs and heard her running behind me.

"Shaela!"

I stopped, turned around, and her face was a mask of concern that quickly turned to anger.

"Why the fuck do you keep putting up with this shit?"

Yana, you have no idea how hard it is to get away from him," I cried into her arms.

"I know it is but you have to, girl. You got to leave him before it's too late."

~

"Shaela?"

Erica was waving her hand in front of my face.

"Get yo' hand out of my face. Instead of you being fucking jealous because she has Kyson. You should be trying to take her and Keisha under your wing and tell them how you got out of this vicious ass whooping's Duke used to hand yo ass."

"He haven't beat me in years though. That first and last time was a mistake. He was on drugs back then."

"Bitch still, he whipped yo ass. Had you in the hospital with two arm braces and a leg brace, oh and don't forget that time he almost broke yo neck to bitch." I snapped.

"Okay Shaela."

I knew I was getting under her skin she hated for anybody to tell her add the truth while she was walking around like she had such a perfect relationship. I had to bring her ass back down off that pedestal. You can't belittle somebody when you were once in that same situation.

"Yea okay. Look I got to go."

"Its not that serious. I'm not mad. You're telling the truth. Maybe I do need to go have a serious talk with Diamond before she makes the mistake of walking down the aisle with him." She spoke.

Everybody go through something that makes them seem dumb to every body else whose not in they're shoes but, truth be told if you've never been physically, verbally and emotionally abuse you would never understand and why we stay with the men who do it.

26

DIAMOND

What Momma Cha said was really weighing down on me. I started realizing I wasn't happy I was just with Kyson because he took care of everything. When I was with him all of my worried went out of the window, I fell in love with him fast and that was apart of the problem. I let him think it was okay to beat me by not putting a stop to it a long time ago. He killed our first child.

I sat in the living room thinking about my decision to stay with him. The things I put up with no woman should have to through especially not with a nigga who claimed to love you.

The more I thought about it the more pissed off and angry I became. I deserved way better than this.

Finally, I got up and went upstairs t to our bedroom. Bag by bag I packed alk of my things and put them in my car. I couldn't marry Kyson. It was right, 'll I was doing was giving into him because this was what he wanted.

After getting everything loaded, I gT into the car and drove to my mothers house. I knew she wouldn't turn me away.

I knew when Kyson got home and realized I left him, he was going to tear the streets up looking for me.

I pulled into her driveway, parked and got out of the car.

"Diamond?" My mother asked opening the door before I could knock.

"Hey momma."

I walked in and sat down on the sofa.

"What's going on with you?"

"I left Kyson."

"Did that nigga out his hands on you again?" she asked sitting down next to me.

I shook My head.

"Its just I was thinking about everything he put me through. The many many bearings. I'm just over it. Im not happy. He doesn't make me happy anymore."

"I'm happy you left him. I was waiting for you to see he was no good for you. Even though I wished it would've been way sooner than this. Your happiness is the most important thing. Do you hear me? You don't need a man to make you happy."

"I know mommy. Thank you. I'm going to go lay down."

I got up and went into my bedroom. I laid across the bed and just thought about the decision I just made and smiled. I finally taking Keisha's advice and was about to figure out what made me happy. I also knew Kyson was not going to make this easy on me.

27

KYSON

I was blowing Diamonds phone up while looking at her engagement ring that was sitting on the dresser. I didn't know what was going on with her. I been trying to make everything right between us. I needed her to see I didn't want my baby's mother. I was all about her and she just leave me?

Wham!

I turned and punched a hold in the wall.

This shit was some bullshit, I was putting in the work and If she thought she was just about to leave me she had another thing coming.

I ran down stairs and out of the house. I was going to find her and try to make everything right. I loved Diamond and I know she didn't have to stick with me through everything but, she did and that made me love her even more.

I jumped in my car and headed straight for Sunny Clove, I knew that's, where she ran to, her mother.

When I pulled into the driveway I got out and ran to her door. I knocked until her mother pulled the door open "What?" she asked with a slight attitude.

"I need to talk to her."

"Kyson, she doesn't want to talk. If she did I'm sure she would of answered her phone for you." She tried closing the door but, I stuck my foot in the door.

"Tell her I just need to talk to her please." I pleaded. I was willing to do anything to show Diamond I was serious about us. She was carrying my seed and I just wanted us to be a family.

"I can't guarantee she'll come out but I'll go tell her." She closed the door and locked it behind her.

I sat down on the porch and waited for twenty minutes, when I realized she wasn't coming outside I got up and started heading towards my car when the door opened.

"Kyson. What are doing out here?" Diamond asked.

"Trying to get you to come back home. What did I do baby? Tell me, I'll fix it."

"You didn't do anything. I'm just not happy Kyson. I'm not even twenty yet and I've been through more than a grown ass woman with you. I shouldn't have to go through this not at my age."

She was looking me in my eyes.

"I know I did a lot of fucked ducked up shit to you. I'm sorry. I hope you believe me. I'm not here to drag you home or make you stay. I just need you to know I love you and our baby. I want to marry you."

"I just need some time Kyson. I'm sorry." She said. She was about to turn around when I grabbed her and pulled her into a hug.

"You have nothing to be sorry about, Okay? I fucked up not you. Instead of cherishing you I pushed you away. I love you ma."

Pulling away from her I got into my car and left her standing in the driveway. I felt a tear about to drop and wiped my eye. I couldn't cry. Real niggas don't cry. I lost a good girl bring a fuck nigga.

I only hopes she could forgive me and give me the chance to make things right but, if not I couldn't blame her. I was one fucked up ass nigga and didn't deserve her.

28

DALLAS

Word got around fast that Diamond left Kyson, that was all I needed to hear. I was about to get my girl back. He fucked up his chance at least I hoped so. I pulled out my phone and called her, I was still in New York, but wouldn't hesitate to be on the next flight to Los Angeles.

"Hello, who is this?"

"Dallas, wassup? How you doing?"

"What do you want? Do you think that just because Kyson and I aren't together that ima fuck with you?" she asked with so much attitude that I almost wanted to snatched her add through the phone.

"Did I say that? Damn, a nigga can't even call to see how you're doing?" I laid across my bed.

"Look Dallas, I'm tired of games. I'm doing good." She said hanging up on me.

I looked at the phone to make sure I wasn't tripping. I chuckled and sat my phone down on the bed. I started thinking and it was time for me to head back to Compton. Nadia had been hitting me up and we were talking g but, not about to relationship.

I was good on her. I just wanted my daughter's.

I got up and packed me a bag before heading downstairs "Where you going?" my mother asked with a raised brow.

"Compton."

I walked out of the house closing the door behind me. Getting into my car I headed to the airport, it was a good thing we had our own jet and pilot who was available twenty four seven.

I landed in Compton a few hours later and headed straight for Diamonds mother house. Her car was sitting in the driveway. I pulled ought my phone and called her "Ugh, hello." She answered.

"Come outside."

"I'm not coming out no where. Do you not feel that heat?" She snapped into the phone.

This time I hung up on her ass and got out of the car. I walked up to the door and was immediately greeted by the smell of Gumbo "Jeanette!" I yelled through the screen door.

"Dallas, what are you doing here?" she asked not cracking a smile.

"I'm here to see your daughter."

She sighed "Please do not come in here and piss my baby off. I'd hate to have to stab you."

"I'm not here to piss her off. I miss her."

She opened the screen door for me and let me in "She's in her room."

I walked towards the back and pushed her door opened "You don't know how to knock. My new nigga could've been in here."

"I would've murked that nigga." I seriously said. Diamond just didn't understand how much I loved her. I never disrespected her. I never meant to hurt her. I most definitely didn't mean to shoot her. I wanted her to see that I was the man for her. Kyson didn't know how to treat her.

"Okay now that you're here. I'm my face. What you want?" she asked sitting up in the middle of the bed.

She was making me nervous by the way she was looking at me "I want you."

I was being honest with her, she wasn't engaged so it was no point in sugar coating anything.

"And what makes you think I want you or any nigga for that matter?"

"I think you still love me deep down. That why you answer every time I call."

She laughed.

"Wrong! I answer. Because you are pure entertainment. You want me to forgive you for sleeping with my friend? Having kids with her? I forgive you, but me and you will never be the same. Ever. You and Kyson are two in the same. No, you didn't beat on me but, emotionally you sure did abuse me."

"I know what I did was up. That was years ago. You love my daughter's and they love you. All they ask about is you. I love you. I always will. I don't want you did to me but, a nigga can't leave you alone."

"Its not that easy Dallas."

"I know it's not and I'm willing to put in the work for us."

She nodded her head.

"I hear you but, I don't believe you. Show me."

"You know I will."

I sat on the bed next to her and pulled her closer "I love you."

"I know you do."

"Ima make this right."

"Okay." She wouldn't even look at me.

I got up from the bed, kissed her forehead and left the house. I had a few things to take care of but I was coming back. I planned on doing any and everything it took for me to get my baby back.

29

NADIA

I was enjoying my life without Dallas. He used to treat me like crap because I wasn't the one he wanted. I didn't ask to get pregnant by him. He decided that for the both of us. I asked him to wear condoms so we wouldn't where we are today. Stuck with each other. I hadn't been talking to anybody associated with Diamond or Dallas. I was over that chapter of my life.

My phone rang and it was Erica.

"Hello," I quickly answered.

"Nadia, this is Erica. Girl, did you know Dallas came back to LA for Diamond?"

I didn't understand why she was telling me this. She had some type of obsession with Diamond and it was creepy as hell.

"Okay and?"

I was mad that she called me about that shit.

"Are y'all over?"

"We're us. Why?"

I was growing tired of the questions. She was waiting to see if she could catch me slipping and get something out of me. Nope! I sat back in front of my vanity mirror and continued to put on my makeup. I meeting up with some girls I met at a club a few night ago. We actually hit it off and I thought they were cool.

I walked out of the house and jumped into my yellow 2014 Camaro and made my way downtown to Starbucks for the meeting. As soon as I pulled up, I parked next to a black Audi and got out.

"You must be Nadia?" a skinny dark-skinned chick asked.

"Yes."

I looked her up and down along with the other chick and automatically knew they were up to some shit. I couldn't wait to find out what they wanted.

"You're pretty," she complimented me.

I smiled, sat down, and crossed my legs.

"Ladies, what did you want to meet about?"

"Dallas," the light skinned chick said.

I looked into her eyes and decided to choose my next words wisely because I never knew who I was in contact with. For all I knew, these hoes can be grimy as hell.

"What about him?"

"You need to get at that bitch Diamond."

I shook my head and smiled. "I'm sorry, Diamond and I were once very good friends and I would be crazy if I went against Dallas and Kyson."

I stood up and was about to exit the building when Los and Keisha walked in.

"Hey Nadia," she smiled.

"Hey, Keisha. Damn, you're huge," I said.

She gave me a friendly hug and said, "I want to see you after I have my baby. You, Diamond, and I need to talk."

I shook my head "Me and Diamond have nothing to discuss. That chapter of my life is over with." I was over the bullshit. Diamond could have Dallas. He wasn't worth the fight and I had none left in my body for him. I walked out of the coffee shop in a good mood. When I sat in my car, my phone immediately starting vibrating.

Dallas: *I'll have the kids back to you tomorrow.*

Dallas: *You okay?*

Me: *Yep! I'm over it! I just want my kids and my life back.*

Dallas: *You been had your life back. You could've been doing what you wanted*

Me: *Yeah, now you tell me. I was too busy being a loyal chick to a dog ass nigga. Have a nice life. If it ain't about the kids, don't text me.*

Dallas: *Bet!*

I didn't even respond because he was trying to make me jealous and I wasn't going to give him that power over me. I started my car and took off towards my house. I needed to get all of Dallas's shit out of there.

When I walked into the house, I went into our bedroom and headed straight to the closet.

"All of this shit needed to go," I said before grabbing all of his shirts and threw them into a box.

I lost track of time and before I knew it, the sun had risen. I walked outside and dropped the boxes at the curb then walked right back into my house and shut the door.

Three hours later, I heard someone knocking something over in the Living room.

"Savannah and Zoe, chill!" I heard Dallas say to them as he walked up the stairs. "You moving out?"

I couldn't hold my laughter. "Nah, you are."

He looked shocked as he walked in the closet and noticed all his shit was gone.

"That's how you doing it?"

I smiled and nodded.

"You and Diamond belong together. I even heard that she might be pregnant by you. Congrats!"

"Thanks!" he said before he walked out of the room."

I jumped out of the bed and went downstairs where the girls were.

"Mommy!"

They ran into my arms and almost knocked me off my feet. For the first time, I felt good. I felt like I didn't need Dallas. He was my downfall. Now, I only hoped Diamond figured that out before she found herself looking stupid, too.

30

DIAMOND

Kyson just didn't get it. I was done at this point with the disrespect, the beatings, the side bitches, and baby momma drama. I was over it. At least that's what I kept trying to tell myself.

"Diamond, you good?" Keisha asked as soon as she answered the phone.

"I'm calling to check on you. This isn't about me."

I always tried putting me and Kyson's issues to the side because it was nothing we could do to change the shit. He was the nigga I fell in love with right out the gate. The same sexy ass nigga I thought was so sweet, but he just wasn't the sweet guy he had portrayed himself to be. I was stuck with him now. Even though. We had a baby on the way didn't mean I had to be with him. I was happy with the way my life was going. I was with Dallas and I wasn't with Kyson. Both of these niggas I fell in love with needed help. Something I couldn't provide. I wasn't a therapist and I wasn't about to be they're escape goat.

I found out I was having a little girl today and couldn't be happier. I was going to teach her all of things I learned from her father. How not to be dumb.

I got into my car and headed to my new home a two bedroom

condo a few miles outside of Compton. I needed a new scenery and even though I wasn't far I sure as hell didn't tell anybody where I lived. Rule number one.

Before I could make it to the interstate my phone started to ring and it was my mother "Hello."

"Come to my house. I miss you." She said causing me to smile. My mother was truly my rock through this break up with Kyson. So many nights I cried myself to sleep. It got so bad to the point where I was eating.

I thought I needed him but, she let me know repeatedly that I didn't need no nigga to handle my business as a woman. I was enrolled in college and was about to take the steps the better myself for the sake of my daughter.

"I'll be there shortly."

I hung up the phone and continued the drive. Singing along with Keisha Cole. I wasn't paying any attention and was hit from behind.

"What the fuck?" I asked myself.

I looked out of the window and noticed a masked man now exiting the car that hit me and tried to drive off but. My car wouldn't go.

I started to scream for help but, it was no one on the street.

The masked man was standing outside of my car door by this time. He snatched the door opened and grabbed me. "Please No! Let me go please! I screamed.

I was thrown into the back seat of a car.

Wham!

SUBSCRIBE

Text Shan to 22828 to stay up to date with new releases, sneak peeks, contest, and more...

Or sign up Here

Check your spam if you don't receive an email thanking you for signing up.

ABOUT THE AUTHOR

Olivia Bryant is from the small city of Beaumont, Texas. She's been reading and writing since the sixth grade. While all the other kids were outside playing with bikes and balls, she was enjoying a new book. People always ask "What made you start writing?" Her answer: "Read my books. I love it. My mind makes up all kinds of stuff so why not put it on paper and paint a picture with my words."

Olivia is twenty-two years old and hopes to expand her brand. She entertains dreams of being the CEO of her own company and has determined to achieve her goals, every last one of them. She has faith and confidence in herself, believing that knowledge of self can lead to great things in life. Late nights and early mornings are attributes of her dedication. While she has no children of her own at this time, she does have three nephews who she spoils beyond being spoiled. They each have dreams of a big house with a fence and pit bull dogs and "nanny" is trying to make that happen. LOL

Oliva has three siblings, two sisters and a brother. She talks with her sister Devinn and brother Nick about books of all genres. The best thing was discovering not only that her brother read books also, but that they share similar interests. She's a very lovable person who just wants the best out of life, the finer things, so to speak. Ultimately, she has goals and is striving to reach every last one of them.

CPSIA information can be obtained
at www.ICGtesting.com
Printed in the USA
LVOW13s2259240817
546235LV00014BA/1400/P

9 781974 103355